PERISHABLE GOODS

Also available in Perennial Library
by Dornford Yates:

BLIND CORNER

PERISHABLE GOODS

DORNFORD YATES

PERENNIAL LIBRARY

Harper & Row, Publishers
New York, Cambridge, Philadelphia, San Francisco
London, Mexico City, São Paulo, Singapore, Sydney

PERISHABLE GOODS. Copyright 1928 by R. M. L. Humphreys and D. C. Humphreys, C.M.G. All rights reserved. Printed in the United States of America. No part of this book may be used or reproduced in any manner whatsoever without written permission except in the case of brief quotations embodied in critical articles and reviews. For information address Harper & Row, Publishers, Inc., 10 East 53rd Street, New York, N.Y. 10022. Published simultaneously in Canada by Fitzhenry & Whiteside Limited, Toronto.

First PERENNIAL LIBRARY edition published 1985.

LIBRARY OF CONGRESS CATALOG CARD NUMBER: 85-42608

ISBN: 0-06-080776-8

85 86 87 88 89 OPM 10 9 8 7 6 5 4 3 2 1

To Harrow School
As I remember it, when I had
the honour to wear "the Harrow Hat"

Contents

1

First Blood

It was October, 1926, that George Hanbury and I first set up house in Wiltshire; and, since for the next six months we hunted four days a week, yet would commit to no one the pleasant task of setting our home in order, I do not think we slept out of Maintenance—for from time immemorial that has been the name of the place—more than seven times. But two of the visits I paid stand out of my memory, and, as they bear upon the matters which I am to tell, I will set them down.

In the first week of December the wedding of one of my cousins took me to town.

Now neither Hanbury nor I would have dreamed of visiting London without calling on Jonathan Mansel, whose flat was in Cleveland Row; for we three had made our fortune together and together had proved the stuff of which friendship is made. That apart, Mansel was the very finest gentleman that ever I knew: his ways were quiet, and his address was simple; but there was a natural royalty about him such as, I think, few monarchs have been able to boast.

I started betimes and travelled to London by road, and the clock of St. James's Palace was striking nine as I turned out of Marlborough Gate into Cleveland Row. Except for my servant, Bell, I was alone.

Here let me say that it was Mansel who had taught me the virtue of being early abroad and, particularly, of taking a journey before the world was awake; "for," said he, "the dawn you may nearly always have to yourself, and, since it is the fairest of the hours, that a free man should lose it is more than lamentable."

I had no need to ring, for, when I had mounted the stairs, I found Mansel's hall-door open and his body-servant, Carson, watching two workmen who were busy about his lock. He took me directly to the study, where Mansel was standing before a cheerful fire.

"Ah, William," says he, "I'm glad to see you. How was it you didn't ring?"

I told him.

"That's right," said he. "Those fellows are changing the lock. Yesterday this flat was entered—by some person or persons unknown."

"Thieves?" said I.

"Thieves," said Mansel.

At once I looked at the wall, where I knew there had hung a monstrance. This was golden and jewelled, and, though there was plate-glass about it, I could have forced the case in two minutes of time. But the monstrance was there.

"And they missed that?" said I, pointing.

"They didn't come for that," said Mansel.

For a moment we looked at each other; then I sat down in a chair and took out a cigarette.

"They came for my papers," said Mansel. "And got them." He pointed to his writing-table. "In the right-hand pedestal of that is a little safe. They cut it open and took my papers away. There were fifty sovereigns there and five hundred pounds in notes; but they didn't take them; so it looks as though they meant me to understand that they came for my papers alone."

"Were there papers of value?" said I.

Mansel frowned. Then he moved swiftly to a window and stood, looking down upon the street. So he stayed for some moments, because, I am sure, he would not trust his voice.

Presently—

"They were of interest," he said, "to no one but me."

I was concerned, for Mansel was plainly moved, and, though I knew no more than the man in the moon the nature of the stolen papers, I had never before seen him betray himself.

At length—

"What's to be done?" said I.

"Nothing," said Mansel, turning. "But, as you know, Chandos, I have a dangerous enemy, and, if he should study those papers, he might see a line of attack which would hit me hard."

"Us," I said quickly.

"Us," said Mansel, and smiled.

And there we left the business, for that was clearly his will; but, though we spoke of it no more, I could not get it out of my mind, for I knew as well as did Mansel that the theft was the work of "Rose" Noble and that it was not to be thought of that he would fail to perceive the significance of his spoil.

Rose Noble was a sinister man, and, though he came but seldom into the light, was undoubtedly concerned in some of the greatest robberies of his time. He was never taken, and the police of more than one country feared his name, for he had a reputation so evil as to be almost fabulous and was commonly believed by those who knew him to be gifted with second sight. That he deserved this fame I can testify, for Mansel, Hanbury and I had made our fortune in his teeth: we had more than one brush with him and found him a monster of iniquity, bold, swift and strong, in whom there was no pity at all. I do not say that he had second sight; but his instinct was supernatural, and I do not think that any living being could deceive this terrible man.

Now, had we not made our fortune, Rose Noble would have made his; and, since nine hundred thousand pounds is a huge sum of money to forego, I was not greatly surprised that he was, so to speak, returning to the charge; and, as it was Mansel that had captained our enterprise, it was, I suppose, natural that Rose Noble should pitch upon him. How he would use the papers which he had stolen I could not think, but Mansel had said plainly that they could be turned to his hurt, and his demeanour had shown me that this hurt might be very sore.

On my return to Maintenance I told George Hanbury my news, to find that he shared my concern; but, since Mansel had promised to apprise us if trouble came, yet week after week went by and brought no message, we began to believe our apprehension baseless and the robbery nothing more signal than a flash in the pan.

It was early in the following April that Hanbury and I spent three fine days at White Ladies in the New Forest, that is to say, at Mansel's country home. This he shared with his cousins, whose name was Pleydell. It was not our first visit, but the Pleydells were absent when we had been there before, and, though the four Sargents in the gallery had told us what to expect, I do not think that either of us believed that all five members of one family could prove so charming.

Adèle Pleydell was the youngest and had married Captain Pleydell five years before; I learned later that she was American by birth. She and her husband seemed very young for their age. Major and Daphne Pleydell were clearly older and were by one consent treated as the heads of the house. Yet all were equal; and, when once Adèle Pleydell affirmed that she was an interloper and the only one of them whose ancestors

4

had not known White Ladies, there was an amicable uproar, an Major Pleydell said gravely, "That I regard as one of the misfortunes of our House."

She was a tall, slim girl, very graceful and wonderfuly and beautifully made. Her face was lovely; her thick, dark hair, lustrous; the light in her fine, brown eyes, a glorious thing. She was quiet, yet tireless and seemed to do all things well; she could drive a car and could ride with any man; yet she was always maidenly and looked as delicate a-cock-horse as when, in silk and satin, she sat to a piano and lifted her exquisite voice. She was naturally eager and responsive, and I shall always see her, as did Sargent—with her beautiful lips parted and her soft, brown eyes alight.

If the others were less attractive, that was no fault of theirs, for I think Adèle Pleydell would have diminished anyone. She was plainly their darling, yet did not seem to know this; and, since she was very quick-witted, this one simplicity made her the more worshipful.

Hanbury and I, as was natural, fell down at her feet, and I am proud to remember that she made us free of her friendship, before we had known her an hour.

So, indeed, did they all; and I do not think I ever paid a visit one half so agreeable.

Much was made of the adventure to which I have already referred, and, when Major Pleydell proposed that they should go fishing in Carinthia later that year and then explore the very scenes of our endeavor, the idea was heartily received.

"And you'll come and stay with us," said Daphne Pleydell, addressing Hanbury and me. "If they will let us the farm we rented before, we shall have plenty of room, and Jonah's a poor showman when it comes to talking to himself."

That this was so I proved the very next day, for I

rode with Adèle in the morning at six-o'clock and found she knew next to nothing of what Mansel had done. Be sure I enlightened her, if only for Justice' sake.

When I finished, she set her chin in the air.

"Tell me," she said. "Is Rose Noble the man to take this lying down? I mean, nine hundred thousand is a bag of money to lose."

I suppose I hesitated, for her head was round in an instant, and her steady, brown eyes were on mine.

"Didn't you know," I said, "that Mansel was lately robbed?"

She let out a cry of excitement and checked her horse.

"I never knew," she said. And presently, "Go on."

I shook my head.

"It's not my secret," I said. "As it is, I've said too much."

With that, I would have gone forward, but she leaned down and caught my rein.

"Tell me," she pleaded, "tell me. I swear I'll not breathe a word."

In the end I yielded, and, before we were back at White Ladies, she knew as much as I.

When I said I was concerned, she laughed.

"I snuff a romance," she cried. "Jonah, the celibate, has had some passionate affair, and he's frightened to death that Rose Noble will bring it out. But he never will. You can't blackmail a man for playing the game; and Jonathan Mansel's never done anything else."

"That I believe," said I. "But why was he troubled?"

The lady shrugged her shoulders.

"A celibate sees a scandal in every bow. The memory of the most harmless flirtation is a millstone round Jonah's neck."

Her interpretation relieved me, for I was sure she was wise; but though I was greatly tempted to share

6

it with George, I did not care to admit that I, and not Mansel, had told Adèle of the theft. So I held my peace.

The next day we left for Wiltshire promising soon to return. Yet we did not, though our homes were but fifty miles apart; for with the coming of summer there was much to be done at Maintenance, and, though the hunting was over, we had our hands full.

The Pleydells and Jonathan Mansel left for Carinthia in July.

Mansel was soon to come back, for he had business at home; and then, on the first of September, he and George Hanbury and I were to go out together by road.

And so it fell out—though not as we had expected: for, though Mansel came leisurely to England, he took the road back to Carinthia, like a man possessed. And Hanbury and I with him.

On the thirtieth day of August we dined in Cleveland Row, to settle the hour of departure and other things.

Our plans were simple and soon laid.

We were to meet at Folkestone and cross by the morning boat; and, since it seemed idle to take two cars, yet send three servants by train, we arranged to keep two with us and to send the third to Salzburg in charge of our heavier stuff. As luck would have it, all three had done this journey before—for Rowley, Hanbury's old servant, had lately re-entered his service— and, since they were all efficient, any one of the three could be trusted to shift for himself; but, as Carson and Bell were accustomed to handling a car, but Rowley was not, the latter was chosen to take our baggage by train.

Not until the cloth had been drawn did Mansel tell us that he had some unfortunate news.

"Boy Pleydell," he said, "Adèle's husband, has broken his leg. I heard this morning. Years ago, not twenty-five miles from the scene of his accident, he broke a couple of ribs; so it looks as though Carinthia was bad for his health. However, there's nothing to be done. He's under a Salzburg surgeon, and I'm taking out thirty novels to help him pass the time."

Here the door was opened, and Carson came in with a note. This was addressed to Mansel and marked "Immediate."

"Who brought this?" said Mansel, taking it up.

"The porter found it on the steps, sir, one minute ago."

Mansel asked us to excuse him and broke the seal.

After a little he gave me the letter to read.

The stolen goods will be returned on the receipt by the Manager of the —— Bank, Zurich, of your cheque for five hundred thousand pounds. This sum you can raise, if you please. No time should be wasted for the goods are perishable.

August 30th

The body of the letter was written in a clerkly hand, but the date had been rudely added, I suppose, that day.

I passed the letter to George and turned to Mansel.

"'Perishable?'" said I. "'Perishable?' What does he mean?"

"I can't think," said Mansel slowly, knitting his brows. "And why has he waited nine months?"

"It must be Rose Noble," said Hanbury, looking up from the sheet; "for nobody else would know you could raise such a sum. Otherwise, I should say that the writer was out of his mind. I mean, half a million for some papers...."

8

"I agree," said Mansel. "It's fantastic. I value them certainly; but I wouldn't give more than a hundred to get them back. If as much. I can't understand it," he continued, taking the letter again; "for Rose Noble must know what they're worth rather better than I."

For a while we sat silent, for there was nothing to say; but I could not help wondering what was the nature of the papers which Rose Noble held and reflecting that, until we knew that, neither George nor I could make any useful remark.

Mansel was speaking in a quiet, even tone.

"The papers are the letters of a girl—occasional letters and notes—in all, I suppose ten or twelve. Their matter is so casual and ordinary that I feared that Rose Noble would wonder why I had kept them safe. They were in order of date, with her photograph, I feared he would think that she meant something to me. I mean, *that was the only explanation* of my keeping so carefully such artless documents."

There was a long silence, and all that Adèle had said came to my mind with a rush. And I could have laughed for relief, but that I knew that Rose Noble was no fool.

At length—

"I still see no daylight," said Hanbury. "He offers you those letters back. When you ignore his offer, what will he do?"

Mansel shrugged his shoulders.

"He may send them to her husband," he said. "I would very much rather he didn't, but that's as far as I go."

Again I took the letter and read it through.

"'The goods are perishable,'" I said. "That's a curious way of saying I'm going to send them to him."

"I agree," said Hanbury. "And it's not at all like Rose Noble. He always made himself clear."

9

"Painfully clear," said I, and could have bitten out my tongue.

But Mansel gave no sign of having heard what I said.

Then a bell was rung, and, sitting in breathless silence, we heard a servant pass to the flat's front door.

The next moment Carson entered, bearing a telegram.

Mansel ripped open the envelope, glanced at the sheet and clapped his hands to his face.

The three of us stared at him.

Presently—

"Tell the man to wait," he said quietly. "He shall have an answer in five minutes' time."

Carson withdrew.

Mansel rose to his feet and handed the telegram to me:

RETURN ADÈLE DISAPPEARED SHALL I
CALL IN POLICE
PLEYDELL

"Good God," I cried, rising.

Hanbury snatched the form from my hand.

"You were quite right, Chandos," said Mansel. "Rose Noble has a way of making himself painfully clear."

I could only stare, and Mansel gave a short laugh.

"Let me do the same," he said. *The letters he took had been written to me by Adèle.*"

"Oh, my God," said Hanbury.

"And, when he says 'stolen goods,' he's not referring to the letters, but to something more—more valuable, *something which 'disappeared' a few hours ago.*"

Not until then did the scales fall from my eyes; but though I would have spoken, I could not utter a word.

I watched Mansel pick up the letter and read it through.

"'Perishable goods,'" he said quietly, speaking as though he were alone. "Yes, I suppose you might call *Adèle in Rose Nobel's hands*—'perishable goods.'"

There was champagne on ice on a sideboard, and Mansel opened a bottle and poured the wine.

When we had drunk, he sat down and wrote his reply:

PLEYDELL POGANEC ST. MARTIN
CARINTHIA ON NO ACCOUNT
MANSEL

And when this had been dispatched, he picked up Rose Noble's letter and lighted a cigarette.

His agitation cannot have been over, but all sign of it was gone; and from this time on until the end, he was, as always, the coolest and most patient of us all. Few men, I think could have maintained such mastery of themselves; but Mansel's self-control was absolute, and, though it was now to be proved as surely no man's has ever been proved before, it never failed and seldom enough gave any sign of strain. Indeed, I often think that the flash of feeling he showed, when the telegram was brought in, was because when he read it, he knew that his secret was ours. Had Rose Noble's letter followed instead of preceding the telegram, he never would have told us the nature of the papers which had lain in his safe, and I am sure that neither George Hanbury nor I would ever have suspected the truth. Mansel was glad also; for, be a man never so reserved, there is a pitch of trouble which he is thankful to share.

After a little, Mansel folded the letter and held it up.

"I am not going to act," said he, "upon the suggestion here made, because, for one thing, such a sum is ruinous, and, for another, I do not trust Rose Noble."

I got to my feet.

"We're all three in this," I said. "That's abundantly clear. If he'd drawn blank in this flat he'd have started on George or on me. But, whichever of us he'd attacked, his price would have been the same."

"That's beyond doubt," said Hanbury. "He's out to recover the fortune; and, not knowing how much it came to, he's put it as high as he dares."

"Exactly," said I. "Very well. My share was two hundred thousand; in two days" time you shall have three fourths of that back."

"Same here," said Hanbury.

"I know that," said Mansel. "Thank you. But it would break her heart. Sooner or later she would most surely find out, and then—well, you can't lay anyone under a debt like that. It's not to be thought of. And, since, as I say, I do not trust Rose Noble, I think it will be convenient to count this document out."

With that, he put the letter towards a candle's flame, but after a moment, withdrew it and put it away in his case.

"So all that we know," he continued, "is that Adèle has disappeared; and, since my cousin, her husband, is out of action and we three know Carinthia as the palm of our hand, we are naturally going to seek her with all our might. Of course we *suspect* abduction; I think anyone would. *But that is all.* Have I made myself clear?"

"Yes," said I.

"Good," said Mansel. "And now please don't talk for a minute. I want to think."

I was glad to sit still, with my head in my hands, for the turn of events had shocked me, and I felt as though I were dreaming some disagreeable dream.

The disclosure of Mansel's secret, the unconscionable daring of Rose Noble, the horror of the plight of Adèle had dealt me three swingeing blows; but what had hit me still harder was the sudden appreciation that thanks to our talk in the forest, *Adèle herself must now know that she was the very lady that Mansel loved.*

What Mansel would have said, had he known this, I dared not think; but I was quite certain that, when he found it out, as he most surely would, he would be most particular never to see her again.

This was no conjecture, for I knew the man.

Full measure he gave in all things, though it were to his own beggary; and that he would falter where a girl's heart was concerned was unimaginable.

Adèle was his cousin's wife, at once his liege lady and his familiar friend: that much I had seen with my eyes; there never was, I believe, so gentle a relation. That the one valued this was patent; it was, I suppose, the light of the other's life. And now it was soon to founder, sunk by Mansel's own hand, rather than let come into the shallows of embarrassment.

The thought that my tongue would be to blame for this most bitter upshot haunted me for days, although, as I shall show, I need have had no concern. Indeed, throughout our venture Mansel bore himself with such exalted gallantry that I have often thought since that, though he could not have known of the speech I had had with Adèle, yet he knew in his heart that she would know why she had been taken and that he was carrying her colours for the first and last time.

My mind being so exercised, I do not find it surprising that I cannot clearly remember all that was said that evening, but I know that Mansel determined to sail the next night, but not before then, because he must have a day in which to prepare for the battle to which we were now to go.

Rowley was to leave with our baggage by an earlier train and Hanbury was to change the arrangements for shipping the cars.

Mansel's Rolls-Royce was furnished with secret lockers and trays, but ours had no such fittings, and, since we must now carry arms, he gave me a note to his coachbuilder and bade me seek him the next morning at eight o'clock. While he and his men were at work, fitting a hidden coffer, Carson and I together were to test and prepare the two cars, so that, with luck, if need be, they could run for a month on end without attention.

Bell was to cross to France by a morning boat, there to buy food and petrol against our coming and to promise ten thousand francs to the officials concerned if we were clear of the Customs in half an hour.

From the port we should drive to Salzburg as hard and as straight as we could and thence direct to St. Martin, for that was the name of the village which served the Pleydells' farm.

That Adèle was in Austria seemed certain, for without her passport and against her will she could hardly be taken out; moreover the countryside lent itself to violence, for much of it was most solitary, and the lives of its inhabitants were too strait for them to intrude upon matters with which they had no concern. I suppose there were constables of sorts, though I never saw one, except, of course, in the towns; and they would have shrugged their shoulders upon any business less homely than a breach of the local peace. For this, indeed, we were thankful, for official notice of the matter was the last thing we desired; this for more than one reason, but most of all because, so far from aiding, it would have put our enterprise in deadly peril.

I have no doubt at all that, had the police been called in, Adèle would have paid with her life for their assistance. The fight was between us and Rose Noble and the bare threat of an ally to whom, if he lost, Rose Noble would have to answer, would have been instantly silenced in the most dreadful and effective of ways. Another man might have balked at so detestable a crime, but Rose Noble was ruthless and would, I think, have slain ten pawns, had they stood in the way of his safety or revenge. I verily believe it was this terrible quality, if, indeed it can be so called, to which he owed his immunity, for, while "dead men tell no tales," it has but to be known that a man keeps that for his motto and those who have to do with him will tell none either.

It was midnight before we parted, and three o'clock of the morning before I fell asleep; but six hours later the coachbuilder was urging his men, and Carson and I were at work. Except that we drove to St. James's and back again, we laboured incessantly till four, but, when I reported to Mansel at five o'clock, the cars were as ready for the road as the wit of man could make them and both were at hand in his garage by Stable Yard. There they were packed and loaded by Carson alone, and at half past six they were standing in Cleveland Row.

Rowley and Bell were gone, so we were but four to travel as far as Dieppe; yet in a way we were five, for Tester, Mansel's Sealham, went with us, and, if he was but a dog, he was ever better company than many a man.

He was fine to look at, very strong and healthy, intelligent beyond belief. Given an order that he could appreciate, he would obey it to the death. He knew no fear, was very quick and cheerful, would countenance no one but those his master had commended and worshipped Mansel himself with the most lively devotion that I have ever seen.

At a quarter to seven we passed out of Cleveland Row.

We made no secret of our going, simply because it was a movement we could not hide; "all the same," said Mansel, "it doesn't very much matter if they do send Rose Noble a wire. He never expected that I should pay out of hand; but he means me to find it hopeless and then to put on the screw."

We dined at Newhaven and saw the cars taken on board; then we turned into our cabins to take what rest we could, for, though Mansel had not said so, we all four knew very well that, until we were come to Carinthia, we should none of us sleep again.

The steward roused me by order half an hour before we were due, and I came on deck to find a clean morning and two or three lights marking the coast of France.

Mansel had told me to breakfast before I left the boat, so after a turn or two, I went below, there to find him and Hanbury making a wretched meal.

Whilst I was waiting to join them, he gave me a map.

"We must keep together," he said; "but, as we can't see ahead, this is in case we part. Don't use it at all until then. I've marked the route in blue pencil, so that you can't go wrong. I'd better take the lead. I shall go pretty fast, but please try to keep me in sight. If I lose you, I shall slow up, but I don't want to have to do that. If you want to attract my attention, use your horn. I'll take Carson to start with; but later we might make a change, and you or Hanbury drive for a while with me."

"First stop, Carinthia," said George.

"If you please," said Mansel. "I hope we shall be at St. Martin in twenty-four hours. We must water and feed, of course, and fill up the cars; but I wired to my cousin that we should be there by dawn, and I rather fancy, poor fellow, he'll watch the clock."

We had already decided that, though we might rest at Poganec after our run, we should leave our baggage at Villach, at an inn which we knew; for not only was this town more central, but to have to "report progress," as we should if we stayed with the Pleydells, whenever we came or went would be intolerable. This may seem a harsh decision, as they were so deeply concerned, but we should be dealing, we knew, with life and death, and that we should be hampered by any sort of obligation was not to be thought of. We did not expect, however, to have much use for a base, but to be constantly moving in search or pursuit of Adèle; and this was why Mansel had been instant that the cars should demand no attention, yet withstand incessant use.

As the boat entered the harbour, we came on deck and presently made out Bell, who was standing with three officials on the edge of the quay. So soon as he saw us, he pointed us out to his companions, one of whom boarded the steamer before she was fairly at rest. I met him with our papers, and, since they were what he had come for, he took them without a word.

This was well enough, but the cars had to be unshipped, and, since the boat-train was waiting, the ordinary registered baggage must, as always, be taken off first. That this would be a long business seemed very probable, for there was but one crane manned, and, as luck would have it, there were many passengers.

As the man who had taken our papers regained the

quay, the main gangways were run inboard and I saw for the first time that Bell had a watch in his hand. A little way off was a lad in charge of a basket and a small stack of petrol cans.

"Full marks to Bell," said Mansel. "They're going to take the cars first."

And so indeed they did—such is the power of money.

Mansel's Rolls was ashore before any of us, and, at a sign from Bell, the lad with the basket began to fill her tank. As the second car was landed, the man who had taken our papers came running out of some office with the document stamped and signed, and, after a glance at our number-plate, handed me back the wallet and raised his hat. Then our baggage was hastily chalked, and, as Mansel started his engine, Bell put away his watch.

"We're free to proceed, sir," he said, touching his hat. "By your leave I'll pay them the money and find you outside."

"Well done indeed," said Mansel. "How long have we been?"

"Just under a quarter of an hour, sir. I promised them five thousand if they did it in half an hour, and I said I'd double the money if they did it in half the time."

With that, he disappeared, and Hanbury started our engine, as Mansel, with Carson and Tester, drove off the quay.

The lad charged to fill our tank was a clumsy workman, so I told him to stand aside and did it myself; and George descended and helped me by taking the caps from the cans.

"You drive first," he said. "It won't be light for some time, and your eyes are keener than mine."

"Very well," said I.

The landing of the registered baggage was now in

full swing, and the quay was alive with porters, bustling to and fro in the lamplight and making less progress than noise; and, since the baggage itself was being swung over our head, I was glad to screw its cap to the tank and to take my seat in the car.

Hanbury picked up the basket and followed me in.

The eastern sky was pale, but it was yet very dark.

Now as we were moving slowly toward the street, I became aware of some paper upon which I seemed to have sat down. So soon as I had a hand free, I plucked this from under my legs, to find in it a dirty envelope, bearing no superscription, but sealed.

"What's that?" said George, peering.

"It must have fallen from the baggage," I said. "The nets passed over the car. See what it is. If it's a bill of lading, we'd better give it back."

As Hanbury ripped open the envelope, Bell stepped out of the shadows on to the running board.

"Captain Mansel's fifty yards on, sir; on the right of the street."

"Very good," said I, turning across the lines.

"It's not a bill of lading," said George sharply.

"What then?" said I, setting a foot on the brake.

By way of answer, he held it to the light of the lamp which illumined the instrument board.

It was a half-sheet of notepaper on which were printed four words:

The goods are perishable.

2

We Take the Field

To show Mansel a memento so ugly went against the grain; yet we dared not suppress it, so I drove to where he sat waiting, and Hanbury gave the paper into his hand.

He glanced at it, turned it about and then put it away.

"Where did you find it?" he said.

I told him on the seat of the car.

At once he turned to Bell and asked him to try to recall every person that he had seen in the last two hours; "for," said he, "one of those men was a spy, and, though we can do nothing now, it might be very convenient if you would know him again."

Then he asked if I was ready and let in his clutch....

The day was coming, but, so long as the night lasted, we had the road to ourselves. Taking advantage of this, Mansel went like the wind, and, since all I could see was his tail-light and this poor pointer vanished with each dip and bend of the road, it was more by luck than by cunning that I managed to cling to his heels. Indeed, the first hour of our journey imposed a continuous strain, for he drove as though the way was familiar, but I did not know it at all, and, what with fear of leaving the road if I drove too fast, and of losing my guiding light if I slackened speed, I wished for the day with a fervour which I think would have opened the eyes of St. Paul himself.

Yet, in a way, this trail stood me in stead, for, when

at last it was light and I could see the landscape and Mansel's Rolls scudding before me like a gull, to follow behind seemed child's play and, though he went faster than ever, I was able without any trouble to maintain the pace which he set.

The sun rose about six into a cloudless sky, and, since rain had lately fallen, the country was fresh to look on and smelled very sweet. Mansel raised next to no dust, for this had been laid by the rain and was not yet dry, and, as the chill of the dawn changed to the cool of the day, our passage became every moment more agreeable. There was, however, a look of heat in the heaven which there was no mistaking.

Our road was no longer so free as it has been by night, but I was surprised to encounter so little traffic, and, indeed, the clocks had struck seven before the pace at which we were travelling had to be sensibly reduced.

At a quarter to eight we met our first definite check in the shape of a level crossing, the gates of which were closed.

To make the best of the business, we halted for a quarter of an hour, and, while Tester was given his freedom, we ate and drank of the food which Bell had brought.

Mansel was plainly pleased with the pace at which we had come, but insisted that now was the time for Hanbury to take my place; then he turned to Bell and asked if he had recalled the people he had seen at Dieppe.

"I've done my best, sir," said Bell; "but I fear there's not very many I'd know again."

"That remains to be seen," said Mansel. "But please try to bear them in mind, and picture to yourself the time you spent on the quay. I expect you walked up and down. Try to remember if anyone was doing the same."

"Very good, sir," said Bell obediently.

Five minutes later I was sitting with Mansel, and we were again under way.

We had now come to roads that we had travelled before, but, though the features of the way seemed faintly familiar, I could not have taken it safely without the aid of the map nor have threaded a single town without direction. Mansel, however, drove with the utmost confidence, never hesitating where the road forked or peering at any signpost, but whipping through town after town as though it were the place of his birth.

When I remarked upon this, he said it was nothing at all and that I knew the way to Salzburg as well as did he, but that he was using his knowledge, while I was not.

"And that," said he, "is why I'm badgering Bell. Bell is observant, and I'll lay a hundred to one that he observed the fellow that left that note. I don't think I did, for when he saw me coming, he probably made himself scarce. And you were behind the car. But Bell and he were both waiting for the boat to come in. Well, there's the making of a clue. It's slight enough in all conscience, but—well, I don't know where Adèle is, and Austria's quite a big place." After a little, he continued thoughtfully. "Memory's a store-room, that's all: the store-room of things you observe. If you're observant, so much the richer your store. But you must be a good storeman—able to produce the requisite, when the moment comes. Some time ago I observed the way to Salzburg; and now I'm producing it. Bell undoubtedly observed the man who carried the note; let's hope he'll be able to produce him—when the moment comes."

We said no more at the time, and, being, I suppose,

more tired than I suspected, I fell asleep.

When I awoke, it was noon, and the day was immensely hot.

Mansel was driving in the same effortless way, looking very well content with his lot and seeming to be perfectly fresh.

When he saw that I was awake, he told me that we should make Strasbourg in two hours' time. We had stopped for fuel whilst I slept, but that was all.

Sure enough, we came to Strasbourg at two o'clock, and at half-past two we were lunching on German soil.

Then I changed places with George, who was white as a miller with dust, for the sun had done its work, and, since there was next to no wind, the cars would have had to travel a mile apart if the second was to escape the clouds which its fellow raised.

The afternoon was made dreadful by the heat and glare of the sun, which oppressed us mercilessly and made the air so sultry that our pace brought us no relief; I never found shade so grateful in all my life, nor yet so scarce, and how Mansel, who had had no respite, bore the burden of that day so lightly I never shall understand.

Twice we were checked by the gates of level crossings and once we stopped for fuel, but these delays were too brief to be refreshing, and I, for one, was thankful when we came to rest at sundown by the site of a little stream. Into this we were happy to plunge our heads and shoulders, and, whilst Mansel and I ate and drank, George and the servants cleaned the windscreens and sponged down and sluiced the cars—by no means a fruitless exercise, for we were sick of the dust, and the sight of the glistening coachwork did us all good.

Night came upon us soon after eight-o'clock, but a

fine moon was westering, and two and a half hours later we entered Austria.

At Salzburg we drove straight to the station, where Rowley lay, stretched on our luggage, fast asleep. It took but a moment to rouse him and lift the trunks into the cars, and I do not think this digression cost us five minutes of time.

So soon as we were clear of the city, a halt was made, and Mansel called the servants to listen to what he would say.

"You all know what has happened," he said. "Mrs. Pleydell has disappeared. Everything points to abduction—by no ordinary gang. As one of the family, I should in any event have done what I could; but, with Captain Pleydell out of action, it's up to me to take charge. Very well. Here's my first order. Discuss this business with no one. We're certainly going to friends, but we're going to enemies too, *and the latter are already in touch.* I've had two letters already warning me not to proceed.

"We're going to drop Rowley at Villach, where he will go to bed. To-morrow he will take four bedrooms and unpack all our things. And he may as well order supper, for we shall surely sleep there to-morrow night.

"The rest of us go to Poganec, and, whilst we are there, Carson and Bell will stay with and sleep in the cars."

Then he told Carson to drive and called for Tester, and a moment later we were moving again.

All of us knew the way now, so there was no thought of leading or being led, and though I remember little—for Hanbury was driving and I slept most of the way—I know that we stopped at Villach, to find the inn shut, that the landlord looked out of the window, with an old-fashioned cap on his head and that, when he saw who it was, he began to cry to his household that at last his luck had turned, for the best guests he ever had had were come again.

We were gone, however, before he had opened the door, leaving Rowley in the midst of luggage, with his hand to his hat.

We were now in most handsome country, very mountainous and closely wooded, with streams and pastures lying in every dale; the air was most soft and rich, and plainly suited the engines, for the cars sailed over the hills like giants refreshed.

We swept through St. Martin, to hear the church clock strike one, and ten minutes later sighted a long low house, lying in the lap of a meadow, with rising woods behind.

This was Poganec; and I well remember remarking how fantastic a picture it made, for the moonlight was all about it and made all its windows were open and lights burning in every room.

It was, I suppose, ten minutes before Mansel came to a window upon the first floor.

"Will you two come up?" he said.

The front door was open, and Hanbury and I passed in.

Major Pleydell met us at the top of the stairs and brought us into a room at the back of the house.

Daphne Pleydell rose to greet us, and her brother, propped with pillows, called to us from the bed. Beside him sat Mansel.

As I went to take his hand—

"Jonah can drive, can't he?" he said with a smile.

Before I could answer—for I had some sort of condolence upon my tongue—he began to speak of the cars, reciting their qualities with judgment and remembering runs he had taken against the clock and, so, making smooth an encounter which I had been dreading more than I care to admit.

"I've often followed Jonah," he concluded, "but I've never had to chase him when he had his whip out and, to be perfectly honest, I hope I never shall." He laughed lightly. "And now sit down, you two—anywhere except on my leg—and Berry will bring you some beer. I think you've earned it."

I tried to reply, but the words stuck in my throat.

I could not cope with such bravery. The man was jesting; his eyes were steady and his speech was firm, but the thick, dark hair I remembered was white as snow.

As Major Pleydell came forward, with a glass in his hand—

"And now to business," he said.

"To-day is Thursday. At seven on Monday morning Adèle went out for a ride. She rode in the direction of Sava, a village ten miles away. Her mare came in on her own at a quarter past eight. Everyone turned out at once, but found nothing. The mare was clean and unhurt. Inquiries were made at all farms in the direction of Sava. They proved fruitless. Nobody saw Adèle on Monday morning. The day was hot, and she was wearing breeches and boots, a white silk shirt and gloves. She had no hat on.

"Early on Tuesday morning Fitch found one of her gloves. It was lying by the side of the road almost exactly eleven miles from here, but not in the direction of Sava.

"Well, there you are. I'm afraid I've no more to say."

There was a little silence, and presently Mansel spoke.

"You've had no demand for money?"

His cousin looked away.

"None," he said quietly. "I've got the money ready; it's all I've been able to do." He stretched out a trembling hand. "There's five thousand pounds worth of notes in that chest of drawers. They've only to come and ask. But they—they don't do that."

There was something so dark about the way he said this as took us all three by surprise; and this, I suppose, he was expecting, for he let out the ghost of a laugh.

"I know," he said. "I didn't get it at first. You know, I made quite certain that they were out for money. *It never occurred to me that Adèle had been taken for herself.*"

Mansel started to his feet.

"I don't believe it," he cried.

"I know," said the other calmly. "Neither did I. But you'll come round in the end and face the facts—when the days go by and you don't find her, but no demand is made; when the weeks go by and I'm crawling round with a stick and people are forgetting what she looked like—"

"Oh, Boy, Boy," wailed Daphne.

"—but no demand is made; when —"

"Never," cried Mansel. "Never."

"Then, why don't they ask?" said the other, with the sweat running down his face.

"They will," said Mansel.

The other shook his head.

"What about the police?" he said suddenly. "Why don't you want them called in?"

"Because I want my hands free. If battle and murder will help, I'm out to do both; but I can't do either, if I've got to apply for a warrant before I can force a door. We're six men armed; we know how to work together; and we're not afraid of lying out in the rain. Call in the police and you put us out of court."

"That's right," said his cousin, nodding. "The police

wouldn't do any good." He lay back and closed his eyes. "But, as they're not out for money, neither will you."

"I know they're out for money," said Mansel.

"Face the facts," said his cousin. "Seventy hours since they took her, and no demand. Face the facts, Jonah; and, when you've had a good look at them, come back and try to tell me not to turn my face to the wall."

There was a dreadful silence, broken only by Daphne's sobs.

At last her brother called her and asked for some drug.

While she was pleading with him, we others stole out of the room.

I was confounded by this perversity of Fortune and I dared not look at Mansel, for here, at the outset of our venture, he was faced with a choice of two evils, neither of which, it seemed, he could possibly accept.

To conceal the truth from his cousin was to withhold water from a dying man; yet how could he ever allow that he, *and not her husband,* had been offered the lady back? Explain it as he would, the fact must arouse misgivings in the steadiest mind; to a man in his cousin's condition, it would be plain poison.

Major Pleydell was speaking.

"If they don't make a demand, he'll lose his mind. He hasn't slept since she went. His hair was grey on Tuesday, and yesterday it was white. If they'd only hold her to ransom he wouldn't care. If they asked a million, he wouldn't care a damn. We might not be able to pay it, but he'd know she was safe and sound. But when the hours go by and there's no demand—"

"Where have you looked?" said Mansel.

The other stared at him.

"Looked?" he said.

"D'you mean to say," cried Mansel, "that you've been

28

waiting for it to come by post? Why, man alive, that's the last agency they'll use! *Haven't you even looked in the box in the gate?*"

The front door was open and we pelted out of the hall.

Mansel cried to Hanbury and me to bring some tools and a torch and, in spite of his limp—for he was lame of a wound he had had in the War—ran well ahead of his cousin down the drive.

It was seldom that he took some action which I could not understand; but now I was bewildered, for I knew as well as did he that the box in the gate would be as bare as my hand. Still there was no time to think, and, Hanbury being gone with the tools, I plucked a torch out of a pocket and ran in his wake.

The box was a doll's-house business, cut out of the gatepost itself, with a slit for letters before and a little iron door behind. No doubt it was meant to be used in days gone by, for a man on horseback could reach the slit from the road, but the door had not been undone for many a year, although there was nothing to show this upon the other side.

I held the torch, while Mansel played with the chisel and presently forced the lock.

As he wrenched the little door open, Major Pleydell thrust in his hand.

When he drew out a folded paper, I could hardly believe my eyes.

The stolen goods will be returned on the receipt by the Manager of the —— Bank, Zurich, of your cheque for five hundred thousand pounds. This sum you can raise, if you please. No time should be wasted, for the goods are perishable.

August 30th

Before my wits were in order, Major Pleydell was well up the drive, shouting for Daphne and crying aloud his news.

"It's come!" he bellowed. "It's come! It's been here since Monday. The demand...."

As we walked after him—

"Learn of me," said Mansel. *"Never burn anything."*

When we came to the house, he called a footman to serve us with food and drink and himself went up to the chamber where Captain Pleydell lay.

Ten minutes later he returned, to say that the latter was asleep.

A brief council was held the next morning at a quarter to twelve, and the moment I entered the bedroom I saw with half an eye that the patient was a new man. He spoke with eagerness, and the grey look was out of his face. His sister sat beside him, with shining eyes.

There was no argument, and everything went our way.

All were agreed that the sum demanded was fantastic and that the letter be ignored; and, when Mansel said that we should leave after lunch and should not return, Daphne began to protest, but the sick man inclined his head.

"I thought that was coming," he said. "You were ever a dark horse, Jonah, and dark horses train alone. But tell me where I can find you and send me word when you can."

"That I will do without fail."

It was then decided that the Pleydells should take no action, whatever befell, without communicating with us, that they should accept no message as coming from us unless one of us had brought it, but should detail the messenger; and that we should recognize no one as coming from them but Major Pleydell or one of the servants we knew.

And, so far as I can remember, that was all.

Mansel had already ridden most of the way to Sava and had driven with Major Pleydell to the spot where the glove had been found; he had also seen and talked with all the servants employed about the farm; "and, since," he said, rising, "I believe them all to be honest, though painfully unobservant, this is where we come in."

Then he asked that Adèle's dressing-case should be sent for and packed with such things as she would be glad to have. This we were to take with us wherever we went.

Daphne left to arrange this, and we bade Captain Pleydell "Good-bye."

For a moment he held my hand.

"Adèle's very lucky," he said, "to have such good friends."

"Oh," said I, "the boot's on the other leg."

"Sleep well," said Hanbury.

Two minutes later the engines of the cars were running, and Hanbury and I were about to take our seats, when Mansel called us into a parlour and shut the door.

"It is inconceivable," he said, "that Adèle was taken by chance. Her movements had been watched for some time. Let me go further. They watched her ride out on Monday and met her six miles away.

"Now no one was seen near Poganec, with or without a car; it follows that their observation post was distant, yet close to a road, so that once they had seen her ride out and the way she went, they could instantly move to meet her—six miles away. Very well. Now turn to the window and lift up your eyes."

We did so, to see the breadth of a valley, as fresh and

green as you please, and, beyond, a press of high hills, rising up very sudden and wooded cap-à-pie. These lay, I afterwards found, four miles away. High up in their midst rose a fountain that fell by leaps and rushes down to the valley below, a considerable head water, for the trees could not hide it, and, from where we stood, I could see its unbroken length.

"Can you see the bridge?" said Mansel. "A fifth of the way down the fall."

"Yes," said Hanbury, and after a moment or two I made it out.

"Good," said Mansel. "Now their observation post was somewhere about that bridge. A post in the woods would be useless, for the trees would get in the way; but that torrent commands Poganec; and a man sitting there with a glass could see anyone come and go. Then, again, that bridge serves a road to Sava—the only road thereabouts."

I took a step to the window, but Mansel stopped me at once.

"I hope and believe," he said, "that they're watching Poganec now. I mean, our movements must interest them no end. So don't give them food for thought by looking straight into their eyes.

"And now come and look at this map.

"Here's Poganec, and there's the bridge—due South. We're all going there at once. But Chandos and I are going to come up from the West, while Hanbury, Carson and Bell will drive from St. Martin to Sava and come from the East. We may find; we may draw blank; we may meet our friends by the way." He turned to Hanbury. "Your way will be much the longer, so, if, when you come to the bridge, Chandos and I are not there, drive on round to St. Martin and thence to Villach. If you find anyone suspicious, detain him, but not by force; if he won't be detained, follow him; drop Bell at the first cross roads, to put us wise; but, whatever you do, don't lose him, for he'll show us the way to Adèle."

With that he put up the map, and two minutes later the cars were clear of the drive and were making towards St. Martin at a leisurely speed. Not until we parted were we to let them go.

"There's a road on the left," said Mansel, "somewhere just here."

With his words the turning appeared, and, as we swung round, Hanbury flashed past our trail-lamp in a pother of dust.

Our road ran into the valley and lay in full view of the bridge, and, since anyone who was watching must now suspect our move, we went like lightning till we came to the foot of the hills and a pretty, white-walled hamlet where four roads met.

A woman, busy at a runnel, gave us good-day.

"I'm looking for some friends," said Mansel. "Have you seen any car go by?"

"I only came in from the fields, sir, a quarter of an hour ago. But no car has passed since then."

Mansel thanked her and immediately turned to the left.

Almost at once the road rose into the woods, doubling upon itself, like any serpent, and so beset with foliage as to afford no view of anything beyond a ribbon of sky.

For a while there was no sound at all, except the brush of our tires; but, after a while, we could hear the roar of water some distance away. This grew gradually louder, until it quite stopped our ears, so that we knew less than ever what each bend of the road might bring forth.

It was, I suppose, an ideal site for an ambush, for with every turn you entered an inner bailey of the wood, and, though upon such a score we had nothing to fear, I remember thinking that, where two men were at variance, the odds were on him who came first to such a place. Be that as it may, our ears being stopped, there was nothing to be done but watch; and this I know I did with a quick pulse, for the scene was set for a surprise as I have never known it.

It was soon evident that we were approaching the bridge, for the noise of the fall was thunderous and the pleasant smell of wet earth was unmistakable. Indeed, an instant later we saw the bridge not sixty paces away, and at half that distance a car in the midst of the road, with a man bent double beside it, trying to pull off a wheel.

He was so much engaged that we had stopped alongside before he knew we were there, and, when on a sudden he was aware of our presence, he gaped at us and the Rolls as at an apparition.

Now this was not the way of a spy; and, indeed, it was easy to see that the fellow had nothing to do with those we sought. His cloth apart—for he wore a clergyman's habit—one look at his face was enough. The man was a genial simpleton, in whom there was no guile. And I think Mansel would have gone by, for his hand went out to the brake, if the other's delight to see us had been less manifest.

"You're English," he cried, twittering.

"Yes," said Mansel. "And we were to meet a man here. By that bridge. But we're late for our appointment, and I'm afraid he may have gone."

"No one was there," said the other, "ten minutes ago. And I've been there more than an hour. But he might have come since."

With that, before we could stop him, he started to run to the bridge. We overtook him halfway, for, fool though he looked, it seemed prudent to be there first; but he only sought to step on to our running-board and, fouling the tool-chest, fell heavily into the road.

And there you have Hannibal Rouse, clerk in holy orders. He was, I think, the embodiment of that imaginary curate who has for years been the target of an unkind age. The man was futile. He was most garrulous, seldom said anything worth saying and laughed at everything he said; he was prodigal of energy, seldom did anything worth doing and bungled everything he did. I have never known anyone whose company was so distracting; and the patience with which Mansel endured it was more than human. Yet out of the fool came wisdom, and, but for this pelting idiot. I do not believe we should ever have traced Adèle.

I helped the man to his feet, and, since, in view of his report, there was nothing to be gained by proceeding, Mansel berthed the Rolls by the bridge and walked with us back to his car.

Rouse may be fairly judged by the fact that he was seeking to change a wheel without first raising his car by means of a jack; and, when, perceiving that the wheel was sound, we asked him why he wished to change it, he insisted that its tire was punctured and seemed dumbfounded to find it as tight as a drum. It presently emerged that another of his tires was flat and that he had confused the two. He was not at all abashed by these errors, but attributed them boldly to his being "no engineer."

He then told us that he was touring and cared not where he went, but proposed to stay at Villach and prove the country round. This was ill news enough; but when, after staring upon Mansel, he presently addressed him by name and then, in an ecstasy of triumph, went on to remember White Ladies and how he had attended some fête there before the War, I know that I groaned in spirit and wished the man at the devil. But Mansel was perfectly civil, though something cold.

We had changed his wheel, in spite of his assistance, and were upon the point of leaving, when Hanbury arrived. This necessarily delayed our going and gave Rouse time to remember that he had a camera with him with which he must photograph us all. We protested that we could not wait, but, while we were still protesting, the thing was done. I confess that it did not delay us, for he took his picture as we re-entered the cars, laughing the while like a maniac and promising to show us a proof.

"The man's a scourge," said I, as we sped back the way we had come. "He'll make Villach untenable."

Mansel shrugged his shoulders.

"I think we must suffer him," he said. "He may be of use."

"'Of use?'" said I.

"Of use," said Mansel.

With that, he drove very fast to where Adèle's glove had been found, and set us all to seeking some mark of a tire; "for here," he said, "I am certain that she changed from one car to another and, while she did so, contrived to drop her glove, for they would have watched her too closely to let her throw it out as she went."

In proof of this, he showed us where oil had been dripping on the edge of the grass by the road, as is sometimes the way of a car which is standing still.

"The relay was waiting," said he, "half on and half off the grass, close to the hedge. The other ran up alongside, and the transfer was made. And now we'll all work in a line, searching the ground as they do on a dairy farm."

We did so for more than an hour, but found nothing.

Then we took to the cars and drove very slowly west, now travelling together, now parting and presently meeting again, until by evening we had come to a great hog's back, some fifty miles from the spot where the glove had lain. There we rested and watched the sun go down, and then Mansel led us to Villach as fast as he could.

There, more to my disgust than surprise, we found that Rouse was to lodge in the very same inn. Indeed, he announced his presence by springing out like a child from behind the parlour door, so that even Mansel was short with him, while I could have taken the fool and wrung his neck.

I will not dwell upon his follies, the tale of which was enough to make the angels weep, but merely record that for the next three days he continually invited violence, taking the most curious interest in all we did, pressing his company upon us whenever we were at hand and openly trying to follow us when we went forth.

This we did every morning at break of day, as best we could to search the country towards the west, for, to that quarter, we made sure, Adèle had been carried off. Mansel, who alone could speak German, visited the villages in turn, stopping at wayside inns and engaging in conversation men and women whose business kept them in sight of the roads. George or Carson or I went always with him. The others repaired to the hog's back, from which four men with glasses could command a very great view; if ever a car was sighted it was carefully watched, and two would leave in pursuit, so soon as the line it was taking could be fairly presumed. But questionings and scrutinies alike bore us no fruit, for Mansel learned nothing of value, and the occupants of the cars, which were few, gave us no cause to doubt their honesty. Indeed, at the end of three days, we seemed to be no nearer Adèle than when we left Cleveland Row. In that time, however, we received a savage monition that, though we had no idea where Rose Noble was, he had his hand upon us and could, so to speak, twist our tail whenever he pleased.

3

In Touch

When we came in at nightfall, at the end of our second patrol, Rouse was still abroad in his car. For this relief we were thankful, for the evening before he had sat with us during our supper and, hungry though we were, had gone far to spoil the meal. Our respite, however, was short, for we had scarcely sat down before we heard him arrive, and a moment later he thrust his head into the room.

"Guess who I've seen," he said archly.

No one vouchsafed any answer; but Tester spoke for us all, by leaving his cushion and passing beneath the bed.

"Mr. Wilberforce," said Rouse triumphantly.

The name meant nothing to me, and a glance at Mansel and Hanbury showed that their case was the same.

At length—

"Who's Wilberforce?" said Mansel wearily.

Rouse's grin faded, and his eyes grew round with surprise. Then he came into the room.

"He—he said he knew you," he stammered. "He said he knew you quite well. I met him by the side of the road. He asked me the way to Salzburg, and then we got talking and, when I said you were at Villach, he asked how you were."

"What was he like?" said Hanbury.

Rouse described some man I had never seen.

"When was this?" said Mansel.

Rouse said about six-o'clock.

"I think you must know him," he added. "He said that he lived near Bournemouth and he asked all about you and how you were getting on. I said you were out a great deal and— There now, I've left them in the car."

As he turned to the door—

"Left what in the car?" said I.

"The flowers, of course, stupid," said Rouse. I could have choked, but Mansel and Hanbury began to shake with laughter. "I tell you he gave me some flowers. Carson, will you be so good? The box in the car."

With a resigned look, Carson left the room.

"The man's mad," murmured Hanbury.

"No, he isn't," said Rouse excitedly. "He said you were a great gardener."

"He said I was?" said Mansel.

"Oh, yes," said Rouse. "I've no doubt about it at all. We were talking of horticulture and he said—"

"You must have got the name wrong," said Mansel. "I know nothing of gardening."

"You must mean fishing," said Hanbury.

"No, it must have been gardening," said Rouse. "Why else should he give me the flowers?"

Here Carson appeared in the doorway, with a shallow, white cardboard box, fastened with string.

"There you are," said Rouse, handing the box to Mansel, as though there were no more to be said. "He asked me to give them to you."

"I'm sure you're mistaken," said Mansel, taking a knife. "I'm certainly fond of flowers, but—"

"He cut those himself," said Rouse, "and he said he could think of no one who would value them more than you. James Wilberforce, his name was, and, when I asked—"

"My God!" said Mansel, and Hanbury and I cried out.

The box was full of beautiful, soft, brown hair.

In an instant the room was in an uproar.

As I leapt to my feet, my head struck the electric light and put it out; but I saw George throw himself forward, as Rouse recoiled against the wall. There was a lamp by the bed, and I sought like a madman for the switch, while Tester was barking and George and Rouse were shouting and Mansel was calling George to order in a steady, metallic voice.

As the light went up—

"It's beyond a joke," said Rouse, painfully getting to his feet. "You might have hurt me very much. Supposing—"

"How did you come by that box?" said Mansel.

"I tell you," said Rouse, "he told me to give it to you. I understood they were flowers and that you—"

"You say he was going to Salzburg?"

"I think so," said Rouse, wincing. "He—"

"Please describe him again."

Rouse gave the particulars, staring.

"And now describe his car."

When he had done so, Mansel stepped to the door.

"I'm sorry for what's happened," he said. "The fault was not yours. And now please go. We've plans to make and rather a lot to discuss."

Without a word, Rouse turned and limped from the room.

For a little, none of us spoke.

Then—

"Do you believe him?" said Hanbury.

"Why not?" said Mansel. "If the enemy knows we're here, you can bet he hasn't missed Rouse. And there you are. I said Rouse might be of use, and I was right. He's just been of use to Rose Noble. Perhaps to-morrow he'll be of use to us."

My room and Mansel's shared a small balcony, and that night Tester waked me by putting his nose on my arm. I was up in an instant, for the dog was plainly uneasy and I feared that something was wrong. As I passed barefoot to the window, I saw that the light was burning in Mansel's room....

Mansel was on his knees by the side of the bed, with one arm across his eyes, like a weeping child and the other hand full of the curls which lay in a little heap in the midst of the counterpane.

For a long time he never moved, but at last he lifted his head and, when the dog came running, he picked him up in his arms.

I stole back to bed.

The next day was Sunday.

Mansel started for Salzburg at seven o'clock, taking Carson with him, and the rest of us left for the hog's back within the hour.

I ran into Rouse on the doorstep, as I was leaving the inn.

"I must beg your pardon," he said, "for the way I spoke last night. It was very wrong of me. And I feel you were most justly provoked." He laughed inanely. "I was very disappointed myself. But I do hope Captain

Mansel won't take it up with Mr. Wilberforce. After all, we're all liable to make mistakes, and I'm sure he had no intention of playing a joke."

At first I could make no reply.

At length—

"That's all right," I said. "I'm afraid we were rather—rather hasty. Supper's a bad time, you know."

With that, I rushed off, before he could clasp my hand.

When I told Hanbury—

"The man's half-witted," he said. "And I'm ashamed of myself for bringing him down. I don't wonder Rose Noble hangs his hat on him. I think we should soon find Adèle, if *he* had a comic idiot round his neck."

"Yet Mansel has hopes of him," said I.

"As a hat-stand," said George. "That's all."

Not until ten that night did Mansel return to the inn.

We had come in at sundown, and Rouse had badgered us nearly out of our lives, for, remembering our offences of the night before, we felt constrained to be civil, and the fact that the day was Sunday seemed to entitle his cloth to consideration. Before retiring, he asked if he might read us the Gospel. We could hardly refuse, but I fear it did us no good and only enlarged the sympathy we felt for his flock.

Very soon after, we heard the sigh of the Rolls, and a moment later Mansel entered the room.

"Gone to bed?" he said, looking round.

"Ten minutes ago," said I, "by the grace of God."

"Then you're friends again," said Mansel.

I told him how Rouse had spoken on the steps of the inn and what we had suffered since sundown at the hands of the fool.

"Good," said he. "Any news?"

"Devil a bit," said I. "And you?"

"Salzburg's no earthly," says he. "Indeed, I was so sure of that that I've been at Poganec all day." We opened our eyes. "But don't tell Hannibal R."

"He never dreamed you'd gone to Salzburg. If he had—"

"Oh, yes, he did," said Mansel, sitting down in a chair. "But he knew I should waste my time. I tell you, he's pretty hot stuff, is Hannibal R. And you must admit he's put up a wonderful show. Talk about sheep's clothing."

Hanbury was looking at me in a helpless way, and I fancy he found slight comfort in my expression, for he soon returned to Mansel, and I did the same.

"Last night," said Mansel, "you asked me if I believed him. The true answer was 'No'; and the whole truth, 'I never did.'

"And now listen.

"The moment I saw him, I felt sure that he was our man. He was where I had expected to find him, and he couldn't escape, because he had a flat tire. Yet in the first five minutes he played the fool so beautifully that *against my better judgment* I found my suspicions failing and I had to fight with myself to keep them alive. And then he made a mistake. It was a very slight one, and I don't think he thought I saw. He did a thing that no clergyman that wears a round collar would ever do. He put up two hands, as though to straighten a tie."

He paused there, to pour himself some ale; and, when he had drunk, he lighted a cigarette.

"Well," he continued, "the obvious thing to do was to play his game—satisfy him that we didn't suspect him at all. And that's why I didn't tell you. Your undisguised contempt for him has been simply invaluable. I should think he's been revelling in it—I know I have. By the way, I'm telling you now, because you won't see him again—at least, not upon the same terms.

"Now, first, what was his job? His job was to keep in touch. Rose Noble holds a fine hand, but he knows us too well to sleep sound when we're out of his ken. So Rouse was to keep in touch—an extremely difficult job. We were six to one, you see, and ready to find a spy under every hat. So what does he do but step in *under our guard?* It was done in the War, you know; but only a born artist can bring it off. And Rouse is an old master.

"And now for his value to us. It may become imperative that a spy should return to his chief. Very well. If Rouse thought we suspected him, he'd never return, until he had shaken us off. Never. But, *now that he knows we don't,* he'll go when he thinks he's better and never take the trouble to look behind. *And I think he'll think he'd better before very long, for he'll have some news for Rose Noble which will not wait.*

"And now, if you please, we shall all go to bed at once, for I've no idea when or where we shall sleep again."

I had slept very ill for three hours when I heard a car making like fury towards the inn. At once I sat up, for, in view of what Mansel had said, I fully expected that it was bound for our door; but it swept up the street, like a squall, and presently turning some corner, passed out of earshot.

A moment later, however, I heard it coming again.

Again it went by the inn, but stopped, with its brakes screaming, a score of paces away. Then the reverse gear was engaged, and the car shot back with a snarl, to come to rest under our windows, before the inn.

The next instant someone was pounding upon the front door.

As I rushed to the window—

"What is it, Berry?" said Mansel, from the balcony.

Major Pleydell stepped back on the pavement and threw up his head.

"*Jonah,*" he cried, "*she's sent word. She's got a message through.*"

"I'll come down," said Mansel.

But George and I were before him and had the front door open, while he was still on the stairs.

For a moment the cousins spoke together; then Mansel turned to us.

"The man's at Poganec," he said. "We must go there at once."

For all our haste, mansel was ready before us, and I heard him call Carson and tell him to follow with Rowley and that Bell was to pack our light luggage and load the second Rolls.

Two minutes later we left in Major Pleydell's car; Mansel was driving, while the chauffeur sat by his side.

We did not go to Poganec, but, instead, twenty miles to Crayern—the first station after Villach, if you are travelling east.

Arrived there, Mansel descended, and, wondering what was to happen, we followed him out of the car.

To our surprise, he bade Major Pleydell "Good-bye."

"And thanks very much," he said. "You did it most awfully well."

"I wish it had been true," said his cousin.

"So do I," said Mansel. "So long."

"Good night, you two," said the other.

George and I cried "Good night."

Then the car slipped into the darkness and Mansel turned to us.

"You must forgive me," he said. "I'll never blind you again. And now let's walk to the station, and talk as we go along.

"Rouse's room's above mine. I'm sure the car must

have waked him, and I'm sure he heard what was said. *She's got a message through.* And that's the news for Rose Noble which will not wait.

"Very well. What will Rouse do? He'll clear out at once. Well, that's all right, but I don't think his car will start. He'll try to locate the trouble, and so will Bell—they're probably sweating blood now—but they'll only waste their time. And so Brother Rouse will have to take to the train. I think it more than likely that Bell will drive him to the station, for an Innsbruck train leaves Villach at a quarter to three. The same train leaves Crayern at a quarter past two, that is to say, in exactly ten minutes' time. So, if we're quick and that's the station ahead, we four shall travel together as far as Rouse wants to go.

"Now it's all very well to make plans for somebody else. I think Rouse will start right away and I think he will take this train. But Rowley will be on the platform to see if he does. If he doesn't, look out for a flash from Rowley's torch. If, as the train moves out, we see a flash, we leave the train at the next station; and there we shall find Carson waiting to bring us home. If we don't get out, he'll follow the train along, calling at every station until he finds one of us waiting to pick him up.

"Well, there you are. I've set my trap and I've tried to look ahead. I'd have given a very great deal to have your counsel, but I dared not tell you that Rouse was Rose Noble's man."

"Thank God you didn't," said Hanbury. "I couldn't have played the hand to save my life."

"I covet his nerve," said I.

"You may well do that," said Mansel. "Look at that—those flowers. Of course it made you suspect him, but he had you back in your place by eight next day."

By now we had come to the station, and ten minutes later we had our tickets for Innsbruck and were aboard the train.

As luck would have it, there was a sleeping car; and, as this was nearly empty, we were able to buy a compartment which held three beds. Comfort apart, this would save us no end of trouble, for now we could lock ourselves in and put out the light. To insure against interference, we told the attendant to make our beds at once and on no account to disturb us till Innsbruck was reached.

He was a talkative fellow and proud of what English he had, and I was soon in a fever lest we should come to Villach before the beds were made; indeed, as the minutes went by, I could hardly sit still, but at last he had set all to his liking and wished us good night.

Two minutes later the train began to slow down.

"Draw the blinds," said Mansel, "because of the station lamps."

When we had done so, he took his stand by the window and Hanbury put out the light.

As the train drew into the station, we stood as still as death, and to this day I remember every sound.

From the resonance of all noise, I judged the station empty, except for those on duy and a handful of freight. There was no haste or clamour, and, if passengers came or went, they gave no sign. After a little, a gong clanged five or six times, and a moment later somebody slammed a door. Then the guard, I suppose, wound a horn, the engine whistled in answer and the train began to move.

As Mansel was lifting the blind—

"I must be alone," said Rouse.

I think we all started.

"Orright, orright," said the attendant.

The voices came from the corridor outside our door.

"Well, get a move on," said Rouse. "I'm pretty tired. *What time do we get to Lass?*"

Then the two passed on down the passage, and we could hear no more.

It was safe enough now to move and to switch on the light; yet we did neither, but continued to stand breathless, each of us busy with his thoughts.

For those of Hanbury and Mansel I cannot answer, but I know that I was thinking neither of what was before us nor of the secret which Mansel had so brilliantly won. I was thinking how the tone of a man's voice may show the colour of his heart; for the voice was Rouse's voice, but the tone was that of a harsh and evil man.

At length Mansel let the blind go and asked me to switch on the light.

A short study of the map suggested that we should reach Lass not later than six o'clock. The place lay fifty miles from Innsbruck and was either a fair-sized village or a very small town. The country about was highly mountainous.

It was then arranged that each should watch for one hour, while the others slept. I was to take the first watch, and Mansel the last; "although," said he, "I think that may be a short one, for, before we get to Lass we must settle one or two things. Still, I shall begin to get pensive at five o'clock, and so, if you two don't mind, I'll sleep till then."

Then the light was put out, and he and George lay down, whilst I sat still by the window, to watch the landscape go by, very fair and peaceful and, under the rule of the moonlight, like an enchanted land.

When Mansel waked us, I found to my surprise that it was half past six, but it seemed that at some small station we had waited nearly an hour, because of some disorder a few miles ahead.

"Which is all to the good," said Mansel, "for now, when we get to Lass, there will be more people about and we ought to be able to follow without being seen."

Then he arranged that, until Rouse was off the platform, we should not leave the train, and that, once outside the station, we should immediately disperse; we were then to ignore one another and each in his own way contrive to keep Rouse in view. I was not to follow for more than a quarter of a mile, but was then to return to the station and wait for Carson to come.

Rough as were these proposals, I believe they would have wholly succeeded, had not Fortune served us a very ill turn; for Rouse left the train as casually as though he travelled to Lass every day of his life and made his way out of the station without, so far as I saw, once looking behind.

He paused outside for a moment, to light a cigarette, and then started down the short road which served the station alone. The road was planted with lime trees six paces apart, and, as he walked down the middle, we had but to keep to the path to be out of his view. Mansel and I took the left path, and Hanbury the right.

All of a sudden, Mansel, who was leading, stopped dead.

I instantly looked at Rouse, still sauntering carelessly on, with his head in the air, *as yet completely unconscious of the two Rolls stealing towards him, perhaps fifty paces away.*

In a flash I knew what had happened.

The delay on the line had put a spoke in our wheel, and Carson, with Bell behind him, had caught up the train.

Even as I looked, my gentleman saw the two cars.

For an instant he faltered. Then he glanced over his shoulder and walked straight on.

As they approached, he spread out ridiculous arms, and, when Carson stopped, he stepped abreast of the car and engaged him in talk, laughing and stamping and stooping and slapping his thighs, as though he found the encounter a matter of infinite jest, and completely ignoring the approach of a small motor bus. This had met our train, in the hope, I suppose, of custom for some hotel, and, the hope proving vain, was at last going empty away.

Of the little road the Rolls took more than its share, and, since Rouse with his antics occupied all that was left, the bus could not have gone by without running him down. This it very nearly did, for its driver did not seem to believe that the man would not budge; but, in spite of all manner of warnings, Rouse held his ground to the last, so that the driver was forced to clap on his brakes and actually lock his wheels to let the other get clear. Some argument followed, and this seemed natural enough; but, before it was over, Rouse took his seat by the driver and under the eyes of us all was rapidly driven away.

Maybe we were fools, but the thing was cleverly done.

The cars were facing the station and were far too long to be at all quickly turned; the town lay five hundred yards distant, and no other car was in sight.

Too late Rowley leapt from his seat and flung up the road, in a vain endeavour to mount the bus from behind; too late Carson spurted for the station, to turn in the yard; only, as the bus disappeared, a figure flashed out of the lime trees and into its dust. This was Hanbury; and, since Rouse could not have known that he was behind, I think we all had some hope that he might be able by his speed to pull the unfortunate business out of the fire.

I do not mean to submit that we had cause for complaint. If Adèle was not lying at Lass, she was in the neighborhood; our quest, from being desperate, had become full of promise; and we had passed, so to speak, at one stride into the running. Yet, but for the train's delay, we might well have been led clean up to the prison gates and, taking Rose Noble unawares, have had his prisoner out *before he knew we were there.* And there was the rub. To have lost Rouse was tiresome; to have shown him that we were at Lass, and that in full force, was nothing less than a disaster. There is an old saying that a miss is as good as a mile; but, unless we could overtake Rouse *without his knowledge,* we were like to lose half the ground we had been at such pains to win.

Such thoughts and the like slid into and out of my mind, as the cars went about in the yard and, waiting a favourable moment, I boarded the second and took my seat by Bell.

Only pausing to take up Rowley, we tore after Mansel and Carson, now well under way.

Had the town lain further away, we must have come up with the bus, but the road this had taken was crooked and after a quarter of a mile ran into the streets. These were as narrow and faithless as any I know, for almost at once Carson was in a blind alley, and, though I saw his mistake in time to save Bell, the way we took brought us into a miniature market and left us there to get out as best we could.

At once I jumped out of the car and, calling to Bell to follow, began to run back. A passage presenting itself, I took this at once, in the hope of striking that quarter which we had failed to find, but, though it led into a street, I had to turn right or left, whereas, to my way of thinking, I needed to hold straight on. I ran to the right and turned up the first street I saw, but this curled round in a hoop, and, as soon as I had the chance, I turned again.

It follows that within five minutes I knew neither where I was nor how I had come, and, since I could speak no German, I had no means of obtaining any direction. Bell I must have outrun, for he was not to be seen.

Now why I called Bell to follow, instead of Rowley, I never can tell; it was against all reason, for Bell could handle the Rolls, but Rowley could not, and we had left the car so blocking the jaws of the market that nothing could come or go. It was, indeed, so unnatural a mistake to have made that I have often wondered whether Providence itself did not put his name into my mouth, for had I called Rowley instead, we should have lost a chance which would not have come again.

I had walked for another five minutes, without result, and was standing at a corner, where a very ancient fountain was playing behind a grill, wondering which way to take and thinking how childish it was to be lost in a town the size of St. James's Park, when a soft, green fig fell suddenly down at my feet. I at once looked up and around, to see Hanbury's face at a window and Bell's behind.

As our eyes met, George beckoned to me to come up, but, before I could give any sign, they had disappeared.

The window at which I had seen them was that of a handsome oriel, serving a fine, old house, which must once, I think, have lodged persons of high degree, for a coat of arms had been cut above the doorway and each of the oriel's corbels was charged with some device. The floor below was now used as a bookseller's shop, and little but the doorway remained to show what it had been.

I immediately crossed the street and entered the shop, when an old man at once came forward and, using very fair English, inquired of what service he could be. Before I could answer, Bell came from behind a bookcase and said that I was a friend, whereupon I was ushered upstairs without a word.

A moment later we entered a handsome room, more than half of which was loaded with books, while the hither or oriel end was curtained off and made an agreeable parlor, full of light.

George was sitting on a table, gazing out of the window from which he had beckoned me up; this was commanding a close, at the corner of which played the fountain by which I had stood.

"Bill," said George, "where's Mansel?"

"God knows," said I. "Where's Rouse?"

"Down in that close," said George. "He went into one of those houses, but I've no idea which."

"How on earth did you do it?" said I, clapping him on the back.

"I don't know," said George. "I couldn't stand up when I got here, but just fell down in the shop. The old fellow was quite upset. By the grace of God he speaks English, and, when I could breathe, I pointed to *Alison's Europe* and asked him how much it was. He said 'Two pounds—English money.' So I said I'd give him five if he'd let me sit up in this window as long as I pleased. He threw the figs in, but don't touch them—they're the only munitions I've got. And not everyone stands by that fountain; I had to throw three at Bell. And now what's to be done? I know how to hurry, but I look to you for the brains."

Standing well back from the window, I stared at the close.

How many houses there were I could not tell, for they were irregularly built and several were overhung; but the close was shallow—a bare fifty paces in depth, with a heavily timbered mansion blocking the farther end. The place was plainly most aged and would have been a feature of any city I know, but Lass was so old and curious and had been so little touched that the close was no more than in keeping with the rest of the town.

"I think one thing is certain," said I, "that Adèle is not in this town; it's much too busy for Rose Noble. Rouse has gone to ground in some house of call—some lodging or other they've taken down in that close. And, unless there's a back way out, I don't think he'll leave before dark. If I am right and the house is a meeting-place, there's no reason why he should, for he can send word to Rose Noble by someone we've never seen."

"That's encouraging," said Hanbury. "Not that it seems a very popular walk; only five people have used it since I've been here. But it's early yet and—well, there's a man coming now. He doesn't look very likely, but then they never do."

"I don't see what we can do," said I, "until we know which is the house. You can't run after a man just because he comes out of that close. It's suspicious, of course, but we're only six, all told, and, until we've got more to go on—"

"Sir," said Bell, "that's the man. *He was on the quay at Dieppe.*"

4

The Castle of Gath

There was no time to make any plan.

The man was walking fast, and, as I have shown, Lass was no better than a maze.

With one consent, the three of us rushed to the door, and, while Hanbury was speaking to the bookseller, Bell and I stepped directly into the street.

Mercifully a cart was standing not six feet away, and as we darted behind it, I saw that we had before us the very deuce of a task. The man was, of course, on his guard and knew us by sight; the hour was early, and, though the shops were open—because, I suppose, it was Market day—there were not twenty people in view; yet, had the street been crowded, our dress was fatally distinctive and had only to be seen to betray us and our design.

In a flash I had my coat off and had flung it into the cart. I pitched my hat after it, rolled my sleeves to the elbow and, seizing a sack of refuse, which was standing open-mouthed on the kerb, swung this on to my shoulder and started, bent double, down the street. I know the disguise was feeble, but I dared wait no more; and that was as well, for, before I had taken five steps, the man glanced over his shoulder and turned to the left.

We had now a stroke of good fortune, without which I cannot believe that we should have got very far, for it gave us a breathing-space and let me fall back a little and Hanbury and Bell come up.

I had hardly come to the corner when I saw the fellow enter a tobacconist's shop.

At once I turned to see Hanbury close behind. He was wearing a black overcoat, green with age, and the bookseller's hat, which came down over his ears. In his hands was a newspaper, open as though to be read.

"Watch the tobacconist's," I said, and dashed between two houses to tear off my collar and tie.

As I returned a man passed, wheeling a bicycle. His form seemed familiar, and, when I looked at him again, I saw that it was Bell. He had no coat, hat or collar; his trousers were clipped at the ankle and seemed to be falling down; his face and hands were filthy beyond compare. He glanced down the street on his left, and, there, I suppose, seeing Hanbury, picked up his cue and turned.

As I came again to the corner, our man came out of his shop. For a moment he looked about him, but seeing, I imagine, nothing at all suspicious, presently turned on his heel and went his way.

He was a tall, loose-limbed fellow, with a pasty face; he walked as though he liked the look of himself and wore his hat cocked on one side; and, since I presently learned that he was called "Casemate," from now on I will speak of him by name.

I was slouching along behind him, still shouldering my sack, very conscious of my respectability and full of admiration for Bell, when I saw a crowd gathered ahead, where the street bellied into a place in front of a church. This seemed to interest Casemate, for all his haste, for I saw him peering to see what the matter might be; but, when he was nearer, he suddenly turned away and passed by on the opposite pavement, with his eyes on the ground.

I was wondering at his behaviour, when the crowd

began to move and then fall away. Then I saw a familiar bonnet and Mansel, with Rowley beside him, driving a Rolls. Behind came Carson.

Now such a meeting was more than I could have hoped for, for I had been racking my brain for some way in which to find Mansel and tell him what was afoot. Yet, though we were so happily met, I dared make no sign, for Casemate had his chin on his shoulder, and I could not have caught Mansel's eyes without catching his.

Going as slowly as I dared, with the tail of my eye I watched the car draw abreast; but the crowd was about her wings, and Mansel never looked up. I could have stamped for vexation, for Hanbury was shuffling upon the far side of the street, and Bell was already by. Then Carson cried out a warning and I heard a clatter and crash. Bell had wheeled his bicycle into the second car.

As he picked himself up, I heard Mansel asking for news.

"It's all right, sir," said Carson; "a cyclist—" Bell gave him a malignant look—"a cyclist walked into the car. And, excuse me, sir, but you're rather down on the right. *I think you must have broken a spring.*"

That was as much as I heard and all that I wanted to know, for, if, when upon the road, one of us wished to say something which was not for everyone's ears, he had but to state that the car before or behind him had broken a spring; such a statement would naturally call for investigation, and, while this was being conducted, the communication could be easily made.

Now all this was well enough, but, when I returned to Casemate, I saw that he had stopped and was standing under an archway, with his eyes on the two cars and a hand to his mouth.

For a moment my brain faltered. I dared not dally, and the last thing I wanted to do was to overtake the man. He had but to dwell upon my clothes to find them strange, and to walk with his eyes upon my back would be the way of a fool. Then I saw a garage before me and, without so much as blinking, I plodded in.

An engine was running, and two mechanics were busy about its head. As I came in, one lighted a cigarette and pitched the match still flaming, on to the floor. There must have been petrol there, for flames leapt up. As the fellow stood staring, I shot my sack of refuse on to the fire, and a moment later the three of us stamped it out.

Both seemed very grateful and clapped me upon the back. This goodwill was just what I wanted, and after an age of dumbshow, the taller of the two took off his dirty overalls and helped me to put them on. I gave him far more than they were worth and I think this satisfied them that I was in fear of the police; and, when I plunged my hands into a tray of old oil, wiped them upon my sleeves and smeared these across my face, I am sure they no longer doubted that a warrant was out for my arrest. Still, with my sack of refuse, I had done them a very good turn, and, though they looked none too easy, they shook me by the hand when I went and gave me a cigarette.

At first I could not see Casemate. Then I saw him striding along fifty yards off. He was just passing Bell, who was pumping up one of his tires, and Hanbury was shuffling along twenty paces behind. Mansel and the two cars were gone.

I was not much easier in my mind and followed with confidence, for my greasy suit had given me a new lease on life, and the thought that Mansel was soon to be in the background did my heart good.

Casemate went down to a river and over an arched, stone bridge. This was in the midst of the town, and here for the first time I was able to see about me and to mark the lie of the land.

Lass lay in a trough of the mountains, the wooded slopes of which pressed close upon every side; the approaches to the town were hidden, and even the railway line was not to be seen. I have known villages so bound, but never another town, and the dignity of spires and gables so landlocked was very pleasing. Yet, as I have said, I was sure that Adèle was not here, and, when Casemate soon took a way which ran out of the town, to curl out of sight between two beetling woods, I was not at all surprised.

That here, however, we three must make ourselves scarce was obvious enough, for, if the streets had been idle, except for a labouring waggon the road to come was bare. And, while I was thinking how we should bring this about, the thing was done.

Bell mounted his bicycle, slowly overtook Casemate and passed out of sight; Hanbury turned up a passage which seemed to lead to the woods; and I was left. As plainly as though they had spoken, they meant me to bring up the rear.

The manoeuvre was sound and perfectly carried out; I was filled with admiration for Hanbury and Bell; but the burden of Casemate's suspicion was now thrown full upon me, and I was by no means certain that I could carry the weight. I had no cover: mechanics are seldom seem tramping a country road; no man or beast seemed to be going our way.

I continued to walk on slowly, watching Casemate approach the bend and racking my brain. As he turned, he hung on his heel, and after a long look behind him, passed out of view.

My fears now came to a head, and I dared not go on. I was sure the fellow was waiting for me to come up. Yet I dared not stop without reason, nor, without reason, disappear. Then I saw a café beside me, with a table outside its door....

As they brought me wine and cigarettes, I saw Casemate's head appear round the bend of the road.

How long he watched me I do not know, for I dared not look again at the bend until I had drunk my wine; but, when at last I threw it a careless glance, he was out of sight.

At once I left the café and took to the road.

Ten minutes went by before I saw Casemate again, for the way was a natural pass and humoured every whim of the mountains, rising and falling and twisting as these decreed. Indeed, I was afraid I had lost him and was on the point of breaking into a run, when I rounded a corner to see him ten paces away. I drew back at once out of sight, but the encounter shocked me, for it showed how unfitted I was for such an exercise.

But worse was to come.

I had gone, I suppose, a mile in fear and trembling, and the road had begun to rise in a steady climb, when I peered round a bend, to see Casemate *retracing his steps*.

Now I had just covered a fairly long, straight reach of road, and, before I could have retreated, he would have had me in view. This was plainly the reason why he had gone about, for, if he was being followed, here was the very place to discover his man.

Frantically I looked round for cover, but there was none at all. On one hand an open meadow fell down abruptly to the level the road had left; on the other a high bank of earth rose into a crumbling cornice that overhung the way. Only an oak leaned out of the earthy wall and was thrusting a branch like a roof-tree over the road.

I am a tall man, but heavy, and to this day I cannot tell how I managed to leap so high; but, if I am heavy, I was desperate, and, as I have found before, desperation is a remarkable goad.

Be that as it may, in an instant I had hold of the bough and a moment later was astride it, looking down upon the ground. I then fell forward and cautiously raised my feet, till I was lying along it and, though there was little foliage, pretty well hid. The branch was massive and rigid as any rock.

Casemate rounded the corner and passed below where I hung. Finding the road deserted, he stopped in his tracks and, after a long look, turned on his heel and began to walk back up the hill, whistling some air as he went. He paused for a moment beneath me, to take out a cigarette, and, as he did so, we both heard the sound of the horn of an oncoming car.

Now this meant nothing to me, for the horn was that of some car which was going to Lass, but Casemate stiffened like a pointer and stood with his ears pricked and a match in one of his hands and its box in the other. Indeed, so concerned was his demeanour, that I expected him every instant to take to his heels, though why he should fear some car which could hardly be one of ours I could not think.

The horn was not sounded again, but soon we heard a car coming at a high enough speed.

Casemate immediately whipped to the side of the road, and, taking his stand by the bend, peered anxiously round. The next moment he was out in the fairway, spreading and waving his arms as a signal to stop.

I heard the brakes clapped on, but the car was round

the corner before it had come to rest.

Casemate came running back, and somebody put out a head.

"What is it?" said Rose Noble.

I was so much dumbfounded that I nearly fell down from the bough, and then I saw that the luck I had found so unkind a moment ago was playing clean into our hands.

"Somebody's talking," said Casemate. "She's got word through to mother, and Big Willie's at Lass."

There was a moment's silence.

Then—

"How d'you know?" said Rose Noble.

"Jute," said Casemate. "Last night they came for Big Willie and told him that she had made touch. Jute heard then say so. Big Willie was off like a cracker, and, when he was good and gone, Jute slipped up to the station and took the train."

"*And led him to Lass,*" said Rose Noble. "Go on."

"B—but—"

"*Go on.*"

"He's there," said Casemate doggedly. "I've seen him. Stuck up in the streets, with a Punch-and-Judy crowd round both of his cars."

"Where's Jute?"

"Lying low in the lodge."

"Thought he'd done enough harm, I suppose?"

"He didn't bring him," said Casemate. "Big Willie's—"

"Of course he brought him," roared Rose Noble, bursting out of the car. "You snake-faced idiot, what do you take me for? 'Got word through to mother.' This isn't Marlborough Street." He slammed the door with a fury that shook the car. "By ———," he added, using a dreadful oath, "wait till I get at Jute. I told him they'd try to bounce him and I made him swear never to move when Big Willie was out of sight. *Never*. Why did he come by train?"

"Car wouldn't start," said Casemate.

"And *that* never showed him?" raged Rose Noble.

Casemate essayed no answer, but only stared upon the ground, plainly resenting a trouncing which Jute had won, yet sullenly conscious that, by adopting Jute's reading, he had put himself out of court.

Rose Noble ripped off his hat and mopped his face.

"Who was with Big Willie?" he demanded.

"Two of the servants," said Casemate.

For a moment Rose Noble stood still, with his head in the air. Then he lowered his eyes and looked at Casemate.

I suppose there was that in his gaze which shocked the other, for he shrank back against the wall, protesting the truth of his words.

"Quite right," purred Rose Noble, "quite right. You only saw two of the servants. *I passed the third on the road five minutes ago.*"

A moment later the car was being turned round.

I think this short colloquy must show how fine and swift a brain our principal enemy had. No matter how clogged, he had the truth free in an instant, and, though, when he passed him, he had not recognized Bell—and for that he can hardly be blamed, for he had seen him but once—the moment he learned that one servant was not with Mansel, he knew why the dirty cyclist was taking his subordinate's road. That he made no mention at all of Hanbury or me, was, I confess, a considerable blow to my pride, but I fear he credited us with little cunning, but only a blunt pugnacity when it came to a fight.

Now whether this stung into action my mother wit I cannot say, but I know that, as he and Casemate entered the car, I saw at my feet a chance which never would come again.

The car was closed, and its canopy was fixed; the road was narrow, and, in his endeavours to turn, the driver was bringing his charge directly below where I hung. For me to alight on its roof was the easiest thing in the world, and, once I was there, lying flat, although there was no luggage-rail, I could grip the canopy's edge above the driver, for a shield, which is called a "sun-visor," was there to conceal my hands.

In a flash I was sitting sideways upon the bough, and, as the car came back for the last time, I stepped gingerly on to its roof, trusting to my rubber-soled shoes to make no noise. I was flat in an instant, or the branch would have knocked me down, and a moment later I had fast hold of the rim which was to keep me steady and save me from sliding off.

As the car thrust forward—

"Bunch," said Rose Noble to the driver, "if you see that ——— cyclist, run him down."

"You bet," said Bunch, and put the car at the hill with the rush of a bull.

I was not much alarmed for Bell's safety, for I was quite certain that he had observed Rose Noble and, if he was yet upon the road, had only to hear the car coming to disappear. Indeed, I had my work cut out to think for myself, for the road was none too even and I was mortally afraid of losing my place.

Bunch was a good driver and swooped at his corners in a spectacular way, but whenever he swung the car round, I had to fight like a madman to stay where I was, and if the fowls of the air have a sense of humour my progress must have afforded them infinite mirth.

Except for one sharp descent, our road continued to rise or to keep the height it had won, and so far as I can remember we met no other vehicle. Two or three peasants passed, and the sight of them staring at me sent my heart to my mouth; but no one of those in the car seemed to notice their gaze, or, if they did, to find it curious.

At last we came to cross roads, where we turned to the right, and very soon after, we left the road for a drive which led into a wood so artlessly and was so shrouded with moss and the litter the trees had made that a man might have passed it by, as promising nothing at all. Yet in less than two minutes of time the wood was behind us, and we were heading for a castle which seemed to me to command all the kingdoms of the earth.

We were now upon the spur of a mountain, and, I judged, some three thousand feet up. The drive ran straight down the spur, the sides of which were plainly precipitous, for, after a little, the turf which flanked the drive fell suddenly out of sight. The whole of the end of the spur was masked by the castle's façade, and it was easy to see that the building had been set on the spur as the nail upon a man's finger, that is to say, moated on three of its sides by God knows what depths and accessible only on the fourth.

The walls were high and massive, rose into battlements and looked as good as new; and the place had an air of being old rather than ancient and more of an aerie than a keep. It was clearly inhabited, for there were blinds in its windows and smoke was rising from some chimney I could not see. Indeed, I could see nothing beyond the great façade, except a crocketed spire which stood up on the left. A stout, round tower rose at each end of the wall; these were corniced and had red, conical roofs; in the midst of the wall was a gateway, the great doors of which were shut.

I was now trembling with excitement, for the castle, of course, was the goal to which we had been trying to come, but what carried me away was the knowledge that I was about to be landed within its walls. Once I was in, and my presence unsuspected, who could tell what might not come about?

A yard or so from the gateway Bunch brought the car to rest. As he did so, his passengers alighted and passed at once to a wicket, cut out of the left-hand door. Then a bell clanged, and almost at once I heard steps. There was a grill in the wicket, and somebody drew its shutter to look between its bars. Whoever it was must have seen me, had not Rose Noble's head been in the way.

"All right?" I heard him say.

"O.K.," said the other, and opened the little door. Rose Noble and Casemate passed in.

Now, as soon as the car had stopped, I had moved as far as I could to the right of the canopy, so as to make the most of what cover I had; whether I moved again was depending on where the man stood who admitted the car. With one of the great doors set wide the car could pass in, and, if as I fully expected, the left-hand door was opened, the porter was sure to hold it and I should be out of his sight.

Now so much fell out very well. Only one door was opened, and that was the left; I saw the hands of the porter pulling it back; *but the door had been made in two halves, and, while the lower swung open, the upper stayed fast.*

The car was about to pass in—*with three inches of headroom to spare*, and, if I stayed on her roof, I should be swept off or crushed—probably crushed.

Had I not been on the edge, I must have been badly hurt, for Bunch thrust forward, as though he knew I was there.

I got to my knees and jumped as best I could.

Happily I lit upon turf, but this sloped down from the drive, and I tumbled, like a clown in the sawdust, before I could bring myself up. As I did so, I heard the door shut and the bolts shot home.

To report to Mansel was plainly the first thing to do; and, since anyone at a window could have shot me down, I got to my feet and started to run for the wood. Except that I was shaken, I felt none the worse for my fall, and here I think I was lucky, for I had leapt blindly and had not taken off clean.

Halfway to the wood I rested behind a tree and looked about me.

The prospect was magnificent indeed: all around were mountains and forests, rising and falling as far as the eye could see, and, the sky being very blue and the sunshine brilliant, the castle looked fabulous, and a man that came suddenly upon it might well have been forgiven for rubbing his eyes.

How Rose Noble had come to be so installed I could not think, but, had he spent his life searching, he could not have found a prison one half so suitable. The place was solitary and most secure: no cries could be heard, nor any signals seen; the one approach was hidden, and such as found it could not conceal their coming, for there were not six trees on the spur and the wood lay two hundred yards from the castle wall.

This reflection made me take to my heels, for, if I could withdraw unseen, that would be a point in our favour, and we had none to spare. Indeed, when I thought of those walls my spirits sank, and remembering how near I had come to passing in, I could have struck myself. What was worse, I was sure that, had he been placed as I, Mansel would somehow have done it and not have let slip a chance which surely was gone for good.

So I came to the wood, and, after watching for some time for any sort of sign that I had been seen, made my way down the drive as fast as I could.

Twenty minutes later I reached the cross roads.

There to my great surprise, Rowley rose out of a ditch and said that Mansel was waiting a stone's throw away. Then he told me which way to take, and a moment later I saw the two cars below me and Mansel and George poring over a paper book, whilst Carson was feeding Tester and Bell was washing his face in a little rill.

They seemed very glad to see me and most eager to hear my news.

I told my tale.

When I had finished, Mansel put a hand on my arm.

"William," he said, "she will thank you. I haven't got the words. But please don't count it bad luck that you were shut out. If you had gone in, you'd have made a fatal mistake. Alone, unarmed and with no idea of the building, you wouldn't have stood an earthly; and, what would have been far worse, *we shouldn't have known where you were*."

"But—"

"There is no but here," said Mansel. "You've played and you've won your game; but, if you'd gone on, you'd have thrown the rubber away. Do please remember that battles have gone wrong, wars have been lost and the history of the world has been changed, because valour has outrun discretion and *men have lost touch*."

It was easy enough to see the force of his words, and

I have often thought since that the ways of Providence are strange indeed, for, if Casemate had not turned back, I should not have hung in the oak, and, if the castle door had not been cut asunder, I am sure that I should not have lived to tell this tale.

Then Mansel told me that Bell had seen Rose Noble go by and had followed him down; that George and Bell had both seen me on the roof of the car and, while George had pushed on to the cross roads, Bell had raced back to meet Mansel and bring up the cars.

"And now," said he, "to breakfast. I picked up some food at Lass. And you'll be glad of a wash. And as soon as ever we've done, I want you to show us around."

Whilst we were eating, we decided that Mansel and George and I should go out on foot, that one servant should watch the cross roads and the others stay with the cars until we returned. If one of the enemy passed he was not to be stopped or followed, but only marked "for," said Mansel, "Mr. Chandos has done the trick, and we don't want to start a new hare till we know where we are. Of course, if Rose Noble comes by, you will shoot him at sight; but, unless I'm much mistaken, he won't come out any more."

With that, he told Carson and Bell to serve out a pistol apiece, and, when this was done, he and George and I set out for the wood.

As we went I asked what was the book which I had found them reading when I came in.

George pulled it out of his pocket and held it up.

"Souvenir," he said. "When I gave the bookseller his money and borrowed his plumes, he pressed this into my hand. He had a speech ready, I fear, but, beyond that he was the author, I have no idea what he said. Whilst I was waiting at the cross roads I looked to see what it was. It's a guide in English to Lass and the neighbourhood. The grammar's unequal, but, if I could write half as good a guide in German, I should be more than pleased. And it's got a good plan of Lass and a couple of maps."

We said no more at that time, for we were approaching the wood.

This we afterwards found was nearly a mile across, by some half a mile in depth. The drive which led to the spur went to the heart of the thicket and there turned sharp to the left; from there it ran slightly up hill to the edge of the wood and then directly down to the castle gate. It follows that, from anyone walking, the spur and the castle were hidden till he came to the edge of the wood, but then burst upon him in an instant, as though some curtain had suddenly been let fall.

Before we breasted the rise, for caution's sake we had stepped in among the trees, and, when I had parted the branches and Mansel and George had come up, I heard the one catch his breath, while the other stood staring like a zany upon the remarkable scene.

Presently we moved to a knoll and lay down behind its swell.

The spur was empty, and the castle walls bare as I had left them; only the smoke I had noticed gave any sign of life.

"Where's that guide?" said Mansel suddenly. "See if it mentions this place."

Hanbury had the book in an instant and was studying one of its maps.

"Gath," he said, after a moment. "This should be the Castle of Gath. And now for the text."

Hastily he scanned the pages.

Then he bent the book open and gave it into Mansel's hand.

And, since I cannot better the bookseller's description of the place, I will set it down word for word.

THE CASTLES OF GATH

Few peoples know of this castles, because great care was taken from at first that it must be most private and for a long time it was not mark on the state maps.

Gath was builted in the end of the fifteenth century by the great King Maximilian, Holy Roman Emperor, "The Last of the Knights," as he is named by his proud loving subjects, so as to be a tranquil castles where he can retire to rest sometimes from the cares of reign. It was always kept in readiness to receive him and a small suite.

The visitor who will go the seven miles according to the plan of the page 7 will be handsomely rewarded, for the site is unique and the building is posed on the brink of a mountain and seems to be a veritable "castles in the air." It is easy to believe that the great King was happy to stay here during his short respites and in the company of a few trusteds retainers to find peace and refreshment, not to be said inspirations for future glory.

But if one has found it so fine to see from afar, it will be a pity not to visit the interior. This may be done on Wednesdays and Saturdays between two and four o'clock by permission of the present owner, Count —— of ——.

The visiting of the apartments is made under the custody of a caretakers who fulfills intelligence with curtesy.

We now enter by a deep archway into a fine courtyard, with a waterbason in its midst. A spring rises in the bason and flows in a cascade through the court-

yard and under a smaller archway. Let us follow it. Lo, we are in a pretty terrace, where flowers blow, and running all of the length of the South of the Castles, not counting the round tower at each end. Here we seem to be standing on the edge of some earth, for the green cliff falls down directly and the cascade curves over it like a bow. This is the water supplies of the Castles.

We now retrace our steps to the courtyard and ascend the Grand Staircase on the West. The first room is an antichamber, as the furniture suggests, for everything has been left in the State Apartments as when the great King died.

The following was the reception room of the King. The tapestries are notable.

From this we go into a gallery of stone. Here, no doubt, were guards when the King was there, for the gallery is at the corner of the courtyard and the King's apartments are about to begin. This gallery leads into the south-west tower, which is not shown and has been modernized, and another staircase goes down from it to the terrace where the flowers blow.

Now we come to the south front and the King's apartments. These are untoucheds.

The first is another antichamber.

Then we enter the royal dining-room. The tapestries are very fine. The visitor will observe that the room is not large because the King has not entertained a guest here.

We now pass into the King's Bedchamber. This is very stately. The crimson hangings of the magnificent bed and the superb furniture and tapestries, the richery of the polished woodcarvings all reflects the departed majesty of "The Last of the Knights."

The King's Closet comes next.

From this we enter the Queen's Bedchamber, which is like the King's, but, of course, less magnificence. The hangings are purple.

Then comes another day-chamber for the uses of the Queen, and we then enter an antichamber before passing into a stony gallery similar in all respects to the first.

The south-east tower is not shown.

Now we come to the oratory. There is a door and stairs going down from the oratory into the chapel. There are many shrines in the mountains, but not like this. It is still here always, in the midst of the storm. The glass in the panes is unquestionable and the finery of the woodcarving is beyond praise.

That is all that is shown.

The other part of the Castles have been modernized.

It is regretful that, since above written, the owner of Gath has lately died and there is a law-suit for the possession of the Castles. Because of which the interior is not now shown.

This admirable description we read all three together, Mansel holding the book and waiting, until we had finished, to turn a page.

When it was done he looked up into the sky.

Presently he sighed.

"One has much to be thankful for," he said. And then, "Let's hope they let her walk on 'the pretty terrace, where flowers blow.'"

Hanbury and I said nothing, for, indeed, there was nothing to be said.

Presently Mansel spoke again.

"One thing stands out—any chance of a snap division, which we may have thought we had, can be written right off. If they thought we were still at Villach,

73

it would be different; when your enemy's that far away, you're apt to be careless about keeping the door he can't enter and watching the wall he can't scale. But to rush a position like this when it's properly manned is quite impossible. Very well. There's only one thing to do, and that is to go on play-acting.

"If Chandos was not seen on the spur—and I think it unlikely that he was—Rose Noble has a right to infer that when we came to the cross roads we didn't know which way to go. Well, he hasn't much use for inferences, and so I propose to prove to his satisfaction that this inference is a fact. We're going to forget about Gath, and we're going to scour the country for miles around. We shall take up our quarters at Lass, come to the cross roads at dawn and spend the whole of the day visiting villages and farms and combing the countryside. While we are doing this we shall take care to study Gath *from every side*. That'll be easy enough. And to-morrow, to round the picture, we shall discover the castle and drive up and ring the bell. I don't imagine Rose Noble will answer the door, but I'm sure that he'll be within earshot and I'd like him to hear what I say.

"And, if all goes well, two or three days later we'll call again. But this time we'll come by night, and I think we'll let the bell go."

For a little we lay there silent, digesting his words. Then—

"At the moment," said I, "they've lost us. Doesn't it seem a pity to let them find us again?"

"Yes," said Mansel, "it does. But no man can have it both ways. So long as he's out of touch, Rose Noble won't close an eye; and so long as his eyes are open, we shall never get into Gath. So far as I can see, one sentry is more than enough to watch those walls. Very well. Would you omit that precaution, when the last time you'd seen the enemy he was two miles away?"

Hanbury fingered his chin.

"How did Rose Noble get there?" he said. "I mean, it's a private house."

Mansel shrugged his shoulders.

"I imagine he's bought the caretakers. It's often been done in London—in the good old days. And there it was dangerous; but here there's next to no risk. No neighbours to raise their eyebrows; seven miles from the nearest town; ownership in dispute, and no visitors allowed. Once he had found the place, it was too easy."

"I agree," said Hanbury. "And the greatest of these is 'ownership in dispute.' Supposing the disputants heard that the Castle of Gath was taking in paying guests."

"What then?" said Mansel.

"Well, wouldn't they take some action?"

"Of course they would," said Mansel. "But what action would they take?"

"I don't know," said Hanbury. "But—"

"Neither do I," said Mansel, "and there's the rub. If they'd let me take the action, well and good. But they'd never do that. If I pitched it in pretty strong, they'd probably come along with a couple of local police and a lawyer's clerk....And don't forget—whatever action was taken, Rose Noble would know whom to thank. He'd know that I was behind it, and I'm frankly afraid to think what his answer would be. You see, the goods are perishable. Because of that, *we must never let him see that the game is up. It's got to be up, before he sees that it's up...before he has time to hit back...*"

Half an hour later we were at the cross roads.

It was now eleven o'clock, and within a quarter of an hour our plans were laid.

For five miles about we were to prove the country, making no attempt at concealment and courting the observation of anyone watching from Gath; in this way, whilst appearing to search, we should gain such a knowledge of the district as might any moment be of the greatest use. In the course of our movements we were to visit two points from each of which it seemed likely that a man could look full upon Gath; these particular visits were, of course, to be surreptitiously made, and we hoped that they would help us to discover whether an endeavour to climb to the castle by the cliffs could possibly succeed.

Mansel and I would take one car, and Hanbury and Bell the other; each patrol was to go its own way, returning to the cross roads at sundown, en route for Lass.

Carson and Rowley, meanwhile, were to lie close in a wood and take their rest, "for to-night," said Mansel, "you two must drive to Poganec and take Captain Pleydell our news."

"How much shall you tell him?" said I, as we took to the car.

"Only where he can find me and that we know where she is."

Yet when the time came to send it, the note was longer than that.

It was half past three when Mansel and I began to ascend a mountain which we thought must command the castle and be commanded in turn. Its sides and peak were wooded, so we had little to fear. The Rolls we had left with Tester by the side of the way, and each of us carried a binocular of a considerable power.

At last we came to the summit, and almost at once we saw Gath, not directly opposed, but lying a little to the left, so that we could observe the whole of its south and east sides.

I could dwell upon its emplacement, but I should

waste my words, for I have not the pen to hail a miracle, and that is what we saw.

Enough that the face of the cliff was "produced" in the castle walls, and that Gath was the crown upon a crag that no man could ever scale.

So much the naked eye showed us.

It was the binoculars that showed us Adèle.

She was standing on the little terrace, with her hands on the balustrade. Whether she was watched I cannot say, but she was alone. Below her was the leaping cascade, and, behind, an archway, framing a door that was shut. She was standing very still; her head was up, and her eyes lifted to the peak upon which we stood.

Mansel tore off his wrist-watch, ripped its case open and thrust the watch into my hand.

"Flash it in the sun," he said, clapping the glasses to his eyes. "If she sees it, she'll understand."

The silver was bright as a mirror, and, while Mansel watched her, I twitched the case to and fro.

At last—

"She's seen it," he said. "Now flash it six times, and cover it up with your hand between each flash."

I did so.

"Now flash it once more," said Mansel "And then cover up."

I did as he said.

After what seemed a long time—

"Flash it again," said he.

I did so; and, after a little, he told me to pocket the watch.

At last he put down his glasses and wiped the sweat from his face.

"She saw the signals," he said. "She raised her hand. When you had acknowledged her gesture, she turned away. She's—very wise."

"Has she gone?"

He nodded.

"She went up the staircase into the left-hand tower. And, after a moment, she showed some white at that window, half-way up. When you acknowledged that, she took it away. She's very wise—Adèle."

That was a true saying; only the quickest wit and the steadiest brain would ever have done so well. I think her heart must have leapt, but she took no needless risk. One wave of her hand, and then—straight to her quarters to show us where she was lodged. And that was all. She had no more to tell us, and the game was a dangerous one. The sooner it was done, the better for all concerned.

And here for the first time I saw how well and truly she and Mansel were matched. They were made of the same fine substance, a little higher than their fellows, and could speak a common language which others did not know. And, as Mansel and I lay there, on the edge of the great gulf fixed between us and Gath, I remember wondering whether, could she have done so, Adèle would have kept such letters as she had received from him.

At sundown we joined the others at the cross roads, and within the hour we sat down to supper at Lass.

When they had eaten, Carson and Rowley left for Poganec, taking a note with them.

This was brief, for Mansel was a man of few words.

September 6th
10 p.m.

I know where Adèle is confined and saw her to-day from a distance. She seemed to be well. I am glad to say that I managed to attract her attention, and she now knows that help is at hand. I have reason to think that she is comfortably lodged. If need be, I can be found at the Three Kings Hotel, Lass. Please destroy this note and communicate its contents to no one but Daphne and Berry alone.

5

Mansel Takes off the Gloves

At ten o'clock the next morning Mansel, Carson and I visited the Castle of Gath.

From first to last this visit had been closely rehearsed, so that even a spy in the wood would not, I think, have suspected that we were play-acting.

Indeed, the play began some miles away, for we first seemed to notice the drive, as we were returning to the cross roads after a thirty-mile run. After due hesitation we determined to see whither it led....

At the sight of the Castle we stopped, as anyone would have done, and were plainly uncertain whether or no to proceed; but, after a little discussion, I drove the car down the spur and drew up before the gateway in a perfectly natural way. Then Carson opened a door, and Mansel got out.

When he had rung, he stood waiting, with a hand on the great stone jamb, while Carson, with his hands behind him stood leaning against a wing, and I pulled out tobacco and started to fill a pipe.

I shall never forget those moments or how hard it was to keep cool. Eyes were upon us, watching each breath we drew; it was likely that we were covered and certain that we were at the mercy of those we were seeking to dupe. What was about to happen, no one could tell. For once Rose Noble was dealing, and, whatever the cards he dealt us, with those we should have to play.

The day was very fine, and a gentle breeze was blowing across the spur; except for the whisper of the engine, there was no sound; and I remember thinking how gay the greenwood looked in the brave sunshine and how black the clean-cut shadow which the battlements threw upon the turf.

After a little, Mansel rang again.

For an age we waited; then I heard a step on the pavement and the click of a lock. Then two bolts were drawn, the wicket swung open, and a woman put out her head.

"Good-day," said Mansel, using German. "What's the name of this place?"

"The Castle of Gath, sir."

"Who lives here?"

"No one, sir. My husband and I are the caretakers."

"D'you know if it's for sale?"

The woman shook her head.

"It's not for sale, sir."

"Which is the castle hereabouts which is for sale?"

"I have no idea, sir."

"Well, there's one somewhere," said Mansel, "not very far from here. It belongs to an English lady, who's out of her mind. She drives about in a car without any hat, and she has male nurses with her wherever she goes. Surely you've heard her spoken of?"

"No, sir," said the woman, evenly.

"A big, closed car, painted grey. Sometimes the nurses use it when she is ill."

The woman shook her head.

"You surprise me," said Mansel. "It's common talk down in Lass."

The woman shrugged her shoulders.

"In Lass, perhaps, but we are so isolated here."

"I wonder if your husband could help me."

"I fear he is out, sir. But I do not think he would know."

"Which way has he gone?" said Mansel.

The woman mentioned a hamlet four miles away.

"Perhaps I shall meet him," said Mansel. "But ask him about this grey car when he comes in."

"I will, sir."

"And the castle, or house, somewhere round about here. And, if he thinks he can help me, send him to The Three Kings at Lass."

"I will, sir."

Mansel gave her money and returned to the car.

"Nothing doing," he said shortly. "I was afraid it was useless. Too much off the beaten track."

As he spoke, the wicket was shut, and the bolts were shot.

"Let's have a look at the map," said Mansel.

I gave him the sheet.

As I did so, the sharp clack of wood striking wood came from the door. We all looked round—naturally enough. *Someone had drawn the shutter which masked the grill.* No doubt they would have done so in silence; but the shutter, I suppose, resisted, and then gave way with a rush.

Mansel laughed.

"Seeing us off the premises," he said. He returned to the map. "There's the village she spoke of; we might as well go that way." He began to fold up the map and turned to the door. "By the way," he said, using German, "was your husband on foot?"

As he spoke, he stepped to the grill, pocketing the map as he went.

No answer was given.

With his hand in his pocket Mansel peered through the bars.

"I say," he said. "My good lady...."

No one replied.

"Come on," said I. "She's scared."

Mansel took his hand from his pocket and turned away.

"That's the worst of these people," he said. "No sense, no observation and an inherent fear that you're trying to do them down."

With that, he got into the car.

Carson followed, and I drove slowly away. No until we were five miles off did Mansel open his mouth.

Rose Nobel was there all the time. On the woman's left. He was standing with his back to the doors, with his arms folded and a pistol in his right hand. I could see him in the glass of a lantern that hangs from the archway roof; its sides were tilted, and it couldn't have been better placed.

"It was he that drew the shutter and stood looking out; that's an assumption, of course; but I'm sure it's correct. I went back in the hope that he'd stay there—to laugh in my face. But he very properly didn't. He resisted a great temptation and thereby saved his life. He wouldn't have expected a bullet, and I don't think I could have missed. When he saw me coming, he stooped. If he'd moved, I should have heard him; so he stood where he was and stooped. And that was why the woman never came back; he was in the way, and she couldn't get to the grill."

Then he turned to Carson and asked him how much he had seen.

"The walls are forty feet high, sir—that is, from the gaps to the ground."

"'Embrasures' they're called," said Mansel. "Yes?"

"I'm sure they're not more, sir; they may be a foot or so less. The first windows are fourteen feet up, but they're very heavily barred; so are the ones above. There's no downpipe at all and no ledges that you could hold."

"Then we must have a ladder?"

"Three, sir. Each twelve feet long. The first hooks on to the bars of a window fourteen feet up; the second on to the bars of a window above; and the third to the top of the wall."

"Very good," said Mansel. "Are the windows above each other?"

"No, sir. Clear by about a foot. But you go up the left of the first and the right of the one above. There's a gap—embrasure—directly between the two."

"I see," said Mansel. "Wrought-iron, one-pole ladders, made by a village smith: ends and rungs covered with rubber tubing, so that they make no noise."

"I hadn't thought of that, sir."

"You would have," said Mansel. "Once they're in place, it'll be like going upstairs."

"A rough night would help, sir."

"We must hope for one," said Mansel, "in two days' time. And now, Chandos, let me drive. We must find a forge; and it's got to be forty miles off."

The tale we told the smith is of no consequence; the ladders were simple to make, and Mansel's directions were clear; we were to find the work done by the evening of the following day.

Then Mansel found a rope factory and purchased a quantity of rope, after which we drove to some town, whose name I forget, where we bought what else we had need of to aid our assault. All this gear we presently hid in a dell—a pretty, private place, high up in the fold of a mountain, some ten miles by road from Gath.

There we could work upon it during the next two days, and thence take it direct to the Castle when the moment came.

Of foul weather we had not much hope, for the sky was clean, and Mansel's barometer set fair: "however," said he, "I'm not going to wait anymore. At two on Friday morning we're going over the top; even if we don't get Adèle, we shall see the inside of that rat-trap, and that'll be devilish useful next time we come."

How much we were nowadays watched I do not know. A spy can go out, but he is plainly useless unless he can later come in; and, in view of the Casemate business—to say nothing of that of Jute—I fancy Rose Noble was shy of sending his subordinates further than the edge of the wood. Had he but known, he might have spared his concern; the last thing we wished was to be led to the Castle, and Mansel had given orders that, if we saw anyone watching, we were, if we possibly could, to turn a blind eye.

Now not to look for a spy is easy enough; yet, because, perhaps, we did not want him, Fate must needs deliver one into our hands.

This was the way of it.

Both cars left Lass the next morning at eight o'clock. We were bound for the dell, where there was work to be done. Hitherto, on reaching the cross roads, the cars had gone different ways; but to-day both took the road out of which ran the drive which served Gath, so that, if someone was watching, he should be able for once to account for us all. Mansel was leading, and I was sitting with Hanbury, who was driving the second car.

No doubt our ways were known; but, be that as it may, when Mansel had swept past the drive, a man rose out of the bushes, stepped to the edge of the road and stood watching the car out of sight.

To ignore him was out of the question; we were less than a hundred yards off. If he ran, we were bound to give chase; and we were three to one. We might contrive to lose him, but you cannot run through a wood without declaring your line, and, unless he had a fair start, such a failure would be instantly suspected, if not by the spy, by Rose Noble, the moment he made his report.

"Take him aboard," said George. "It's the only way."

That this was so became increasingly clear, for we made no manner of sound, and the man was absorbed in his view of Mansel's car. Indeed, I had no time to think and barely enough to act. The man had no time to do either.

As we passed, I took him by the neck, and Bell leaned out behind me and dragged his legs into the car.

Not until then did I see that it was Jute.

He did not attempt to struggle; but I held him as I had seized him, till Bell had strapped together his ankles and wrists. Then we took a pistol from his pocket and put him on the floor of the car. And so we had meant to leave him, but such was his criticism of our conduct that after a little we gagged him with a handful of cotton waste.

"Understand this," said Mansel. "It's entirely your fault that you're here. Chandos would have ignored you, but you didn't give him a chance. You served your turn very well, but I finished with you at Lass. A man of your parts should have known that and have taken the greatest care to keep out of my way."

Jute made no answer, and presently Mansel went on.

"I have no time for a prisoner, for prisoners must be watered and fed. So I'm going to do one of two things. Which I do will depend upon you. Either I return you to Rose Noble, or else I hang you by the neck."

"Murder?" said Jute, and laughed.

"Murder," said Mansel, beginning to fill a pipe.

I glanced around the dell.

The spot was peaceful: a gurgling brook, a little lawn and the shade of spreading trees made it seem fit for a shepherd's piping match. Jute and all of us looked curiously out of place.

Perhaps, because of this, I had a strange feeling that I should presently awake and find that I had been dreaming, and to this day, recalling the happenings of that sunshiny morning, I seem to be remembering some vision rather than a downright business of life and death.

Mansel was speaking.

"Now, if I return you to Rose Noble, I shall take you up to the Castle and watch you go in. That is, if it's dark. If it's during the day, I shall watch from the wood. You see, I don't want to be seen."

Jute's face was a study.

"Now, in view of what Rose Noble said when you reported, after you had 'led me to Lass'—I saw Jute start—"I imagine your next meeting will be even less cordial—*unless you return precisely when you are expected and say nothing of having met me*. I mean, he might easily argue that you had 'led me to' Gath."

His eyes upon Mansel's face, Jute was plainly thinking extremely hard.

Mansel continued slowly, pressing his tobacco home.

"I can't return you to-day, because I've too much to do. In fact—"

"See here," said Jute. "You can make it to-morrow night. Do that, and I haven't seen you since you went by in the car."

"Don't try to bluff," said Mansel. "It's only wasting my time. You haven't a card. You had quite a good one

86

about five seconds ago; but I've just drawn that. You see, I wanted to know whether Rose Noble would worry if you didn't come in to-night."

I watched the blood come into the other's face.

Mansel continued in the same even tone.

"I tell you this to show you that it's no good playing with me. Bear that in mind. And now to business."

I cannot describe the coldness with which Mansel spoke; there was no insolence in his speech, only an iron contempt, which must, I think, have entered into the other's soul.

"I'm going to ask you some questions, and I'll allow you one lie; if you tell two lies, I shall hang you from a branch of that oak."

"And you talk about bluff," sneered Jute.

"It's not bluff," said Mansel. "I've got the gloves right off. Two lies, and you're for the high jump, as sure as I'm sitting still. And now we'll begin. Assume you're on the ramparts above the gateway. How would you go from there to where Mrs. Pleydell lies?"

Jute gave a short laugh.

"I thought," he said, "you'd finished with me at Lass."

"So I had," said Mansel, bringing a match to his pipe. "Looks like it, doesn't it?"

"I don't care what it looks like," said Mansel. "But I think you may as well know that I'm pressed for time; and, if you elect to be hanged, I shall have less still, because it'll take two hours to dig you a grave."

"Rake it out," said Jute sharply. "I know your shape. You can wear a gun on your back side, but it'll never fit. You're out of your depth, Mansel; and, if you take my advice, you'll kick for the shore. Your job's to pay and be damned. We've got your girl, and—"

"Carson," said Mansel, "get a rope on that bough. Timber hitch on the wood, slip knot the other end."

For a moment the servants spoke together. Then Bell was on Rowley's shoulders and up in the tree, and Carson was down in a gully with a knife in his hand. The next minute he reappeared, with a coil of rope on his arm....

I knew that Mansel was bluffing, for he was not a hard man. He would have killed Rose Noble, for he was the head of the corner, and, with his death, the conspiracy would have gone. He would have killed anyone whose death would materially help him to reach Adèle. But a spy that, when taken, refused to open his mouth, was as safe in Mansel's hands as a priest on his altar steps. I knew he would never hang Jute, though God knows he had just cause. Mansel was bluffing; and I was greatly afraid that the fellow would call his bluff.

Mansel returned to Jute.

"As I said, I'll give you one lie. A refusal counts as a lie. Assume you're on the ramparts above the gateway. How would you go from there to where Mrs. Pleydell lies?"

After a long silence—

"Which way am I facing?" said Jute sullenly.

"You are facing the wood."

Jute shut his eyes.

"I turn to the right," he said, "and go as far as the tower. Then I turn again and walk along by the wall. At the end of that I come to another tower. There's a door there."

"In the tower?"

"Yes."

"Go on."

"You go through that and down steps till you come to a hall. Cross this to the door in front. That leads you into a room out of which runs a flight of stairs."

"Yes."

"Go down them, and they'll bring you into her room."

"Or the chapel?" said Mansel quietly.

Jute started violently. Then he glared at Mansel, with a working face.

"That's one lie," said Mansel.

Jute let himself go.

Out of a foam of imprecation odd sentences thrust, like timbers plunging in a flood.

"I'll see you, you one-legged———...Put it over, you movie king...When next I meet you, I'll cut my name on your back...We've got the goods, and, by ———, we'll make you sweat...'Cut flowers' won't be in it...I'll make you covet the day you played me up."

Mansel put his pipe in his pocket and rose to his feet.

"You refuse to answer?"

A beastly light slid into Jute's bloodshot eyes.

"My answer's here," he said, glancing down at his coat. "You were to have had it to-night, but, if you're not too 'pressed for time,' perhaps you'll look at it now."

To this day I cannot tell what possessed the man.

I suppose he could not forgive Mansel for beating him at his own game; the thought that all the antics of Hannibal Rouse had been gravely accepted at exactly their proper worth, the memory of the trap into which he had so readily rushed and the bitter reception which he had met at Gath had, I think, inspired a hatred which knew no law. And now to be again confounded, outwitted and scornfully reduced had sent the blood to his head.

"What do you mean?" said Mansel.

"Try my inside pocket," said Jute.

At a nod from Mansel I stepped to the fellow's side and took a bulging envelope out of his coat.

"That's my answer," said Jute, "to all your back-chat to-day. And, between you and me, Big Willie, I guess it's pretty complete."

Mansel ripped open the paper and took out a white silk blouse....

I thought he would never move.

After a long time, very slowly he lifted his head.

"Call the servants," he said, "and put the gag in his mouth."

He spoke so low that I scarcely heard what he said; but, with his words, I knew that Jute's hour was come.

For a moment the glade seemed misty, and my knees loose. Then my head cleared.

I saw Jute's eyes follow Hanbury, as he stepped to the oak; then his gaze flashed to me, as I picked up the cotton waste. When I approached, he recoiled.

Sharply he looked at Mansel, and caught his breath.

"You—you'd never dare," he said hoarsely.

At last we had the gag in his mouth...

"This man," said Mansel, "is engaged in one of the vilest crimes. In his lust for money he is not content to play even that filthy game according to its filthy rules." He held up the blouse. *He is trying to win by taking Mrs. Pleydell's clothes from her back and advertising that outrage to make me throw in my hand.* I do not think that a man who does that is fit to live."

His eyes bulging out of his head, Jute fell upon his knees.

Mansel turned to Hanbury and me.

"You will return to the cars and wait there until I send."

We did as he said.

Two hours later, Rowley brought us back to the dell.

Mansel was sitting smoking, with a distant look in his eyes; as he worked, jacketing a crow-bar, Carson was whistling to himself; Bell was wiping a spade with a handful of grass.

The contented mien of the servants, if nothing else, showed that the world was the cleaner.

By half past one the next morning all of us, except Bell, were standing upon the roof of the Castle of Gath.

The night was starlit, but the moon had set.

Each of us carried a knife as well as a pistol and wore a coil of rope, like a sash. Bell was at the foot of the ladders, with a signal-cord in his hand, and Tester was back in the wood, guarding the cars.

The castle was built four-square, as college buildings, about a great courtyard. Its roof was flat and paved and so made a spacious rampart, which the battlements fenced upon one hand and a massive balustrade upon the other.

Indeed, standing there in the starlight, we seemed to be upon some ectype of the walls of Babylon, upon which, if I rightly remember, six chariots could be driven abreast.

Peering between the balusters, I could see the ripple of the water of which the bookseller had written and could hear it fall out of the basin on its way to the terrace and the cliff.

Now the basin was our first objective; and, since a rope provides the most silent path, we let one fall to the courtyard, and Carson and I went down.

We gained the basin and passed to the channel it fed. This was ten inches deep, and its floor was as smooth as glass. I followed the channel along till I came to the arch. This was shut by a gate, beneath which the water flowed. The gate was of iron and exactly fitted the arch; a man might have lain in the channel and crawled underneath, but, no doubt to foil such cunning, the channel was barred with a grating, through which the water fussed. I tested the bars and found them firm as rock.

I made my way back to Carson, and together we sought the rope down which we had come. Upon this Carson pulled twice, when a hundredweight of fine rope was lowered into our arms. We carried this to the grating and laid it down. To its end were attached three floats weighted with lead. With these in my hand, I thrust my arm under the grating as far as I could. Then I released them, and Carson paid out the rope. Now if there was another grating, this would arrest the floats; but, if there was not, the floats would leap with the water and carry the rope down the cliff. With a hand on the sliding rope, I waited for the check. But none came; only a sudden pull told us that the floats had leapt. There were eight hundred feet of cord, and, when we had paid them all out, we returned for more. Six hundred feet more we lowered, and that was as much as we had. The end we made fast to the grating *below the water line*. Then we went back to the rope down which we had come, and at a signal the others pulled us up.

Whatever the night might bring forth, we had taken at least one trick; for, though this time we might fail to release Adèle, we had now a way up to the terrace which the enemy would not dream of and a desperate man might take.

We were now beneath the shadow of the tower to the right of the gateway as you came from the wood; the south-west tower, from which Adèle had signalled, lay the length of the castle away.

So far as we knew, there were two ways into that tower from the open air—one by the roof and another by the steps from the terrace upon which we had seen

Adèle. The windows which lighted the tower were not to be reached, and the conical roof of the tower gave us no hope. And, since the way by the roof was plainly the first to try, we began to steal over the pavement, one by one.

Mansel went first; the rest of us followed, at one-minute intervals. Only Rowley stood fast, with a signal cord in each hand.

I had gone most of the way, when I felt a hand on my arm.

At once I stopped, and Hanbury, who was before me, spoke in my ear.

"There's an alarm-cord, knee-high, two paces from where you stand. Tell Carson and then come on."

He left me to wait for Carson and disappeared.

I was desperately afraid of fouling the cord, so I went on my stomach until the danger was past. I afterwards found that the others had done the same.

Mansel and Hanbury were waiting, when I came to the tower. And, as we had expected, the was a door. . . .

The door was of wood, very massive and studded with iron. It was shut and locked, or bolted, upon the other side. Whether we could have forced it, I do not know; but Jack Sheppard himself could not have had it open without making noise enough to awaken the dead.

And there, of course, was our principal handicap.

The door of Adèle's apartment was sure to be locked; but that we were ready to force, no matter what noise we made; until, however, we were standing without her door, we dared make no manner of sound, for, the instant the alarm was raised, Rose Noble was certain to fly to his prisoner's side and, if he was there before us, to put her life in the balance against our further advance.

There was nothing to be done but to try the terrace steps.

In silence we passed to the battlements, and from there looked down upon the terrace and the sliding ribbon of water that cut it in two. It was quieter here than in the courtyard, where the four walls gave back sound; the steady rustle of the cascade was only just to be heard.

In a moment a rope was dangling, and Mansel and George went down.

That the steps would offer an entrance we had great hope, for the bookseller's guide had said nothing of any door, but only that the steps led out of the "gallery of stone."

Carson and I stood like statues, he holding the signal cord and I with the rope in my hand.

Two gentle pulls from below told us to take the strain, and a moment later Hanbury was by our side.

He put his lips to my ear.

"There's a door at the top of the steps—locked. Mansel's reconnoitring the terrace and then coming up."

I confess that my spirits sank.

To enter by some window seemed now the only way; and we had already decided that, if we were put to such a shift, we must essay some window that looked upon the terrace below. What windows looked into the courtyard we neither knew nor cared, for anyone at work in the courtyard would be working in a four-walled trap and could be observed and commanded from any side.

Now the windows that looked upon the terrace were those of the royal rooms. *They were not barred,* because, I suppose, with guards upon the roof and in the galleries, no one could have come upon the King.

Again, *that the royal apartments would be occupied*

was most unlikely. The caretakers might have been bribed, but they would certainly stipulate that the state rooms were not to be used. The last thing we wanted to do was to force an entrance into an occupied room.

Finally, *the windows of the royal apartments had the world to themselves,* for the towers which flanked the terrace were presenting two empty walls. Of no other side of the castle could the same thing be said.

Now which of the seven windows might be the best to essay we could not tell, but reason suggested that the one which was nearest Adèle should be the first to be tried. This we supposed to be serving the ante-chamber which admitted directly into the "gallery of stone."

It was our belief that if we could reach the gallery we should have the control we sought, for, so far as we could determine, no one could enter the tower without passing through the gallery, unless he came down from the roof by the door which we had found shut. This belief we found to be just: the gallery was the key to the tower, and whoever held the gallery held Adèle. But one thing we did not suspect, namely, that there was a way into the gallery of which the bookseller's guide said nothing at all.

A quarter of an hour went by before Mansel gave us the signal to hoist him up.

As he alighted, I perceived that he was drenched to the skin.

At once he drew us together and spoke very low.

"At the head of each flight of steps there's a massive door; both doors are fast. The door at the mouth of the archway is shut and locked. I managed to pass beneath it, by lying down in the channel and working my way along. In the side of the archway I found a flight of steps—a very steep spiral staircase, that comes to a sudden end. I'm certain it serves a trap-door. If the bookseller's guide is sound, that trap-door should be in the King's Closet. That would be natural enough.

"We can't go that way to-night, because the trap-door is fast. At least, I imagine it is, because I can't move the slab I found at the top of the stairs; but, if we can enter the Closet by some other way to-night, we can unbar the trap-door, and then, when we come by the terrace, we shall have our way in. Don't think I've no hope of to-night, because I have; but, *if we fail this time, we shall certainly fail the next—unless we can turn this failure into a stepping-stone.*"

With that he told Carson to let him have his shoes, because they were dry, and then to stand fast where he was, with the signal cord in his hand. George and I were to follow the way he went.

We moved as before, one by one, and, when again I found him, he was standing above the archway through which the water flowed.

I knew that below us was a window of three long lights.

An instant later Mansel was descending the wall.

This time we used two ropes, one fastened about him and the other down which he slid. When he jerked the one about him, we were to make this fast; and, if he should pull it five times, George was to go for Carson and they were to let me down.

Wet to the skin, clinging like a fly to the wall, with only one hand to help him, without a glimmer of light, Mansel worked upon that window for half an hour. I was kneeling directly above him, but I never heard a sound. Indeed, I could not believe that he was at work, but supposed that he had seen someone within the room and was content to watch them from where he hung. Yet all the time he was drawing the wrought-iron latch—a feat which, had he not done it, I would have put beyond the power of man.

At last the ropes trembled and then swung slack in my hands. An instant later he signalled that he was within the room.

When I came down, he swung me in like a baby and asked for my torch.

The room was stately and full of the smell of age. The floor was of polished oak; the walls were panelled head high and tapestried above. The furniture was rich and massive, but very stiff, and had been ranged in order against the walls. A heavy carpet, much smaller than the room, lay in the midst of the floor, but all the furniture stood clear upon the oak. The two doors were conspicuous, for their frames rose above the panelling and each of them was fitted with a box lock of polished steel.

With one consent we turned to the door upon our left.

Very slowly, with infinite care, Mansel drew the spring latch. At once the door yielded, and Mansel set it wide. Not until he had wedged it with a morsel of rubber did we pass on.

So we entered the King's Bedchamber.

Not even the unjust light of the torch could deny the majesty of that room.

I never beheld a chamber so fit to lodge a king, and all the standards of greatness which the fairy-tales I read as a child had set in my heart were in a twinkling supplanted by what I saw.

The ceiling was of black oak, picked out with gold. The walls were panelled head-high; between the panels stood pilasters, picked out with gold. The carving of the panels and pilasters was very deep. Above the panelling hung tapestries, very rich in colour, presenting hunting scenes. The bedstead was four-posted: each of the posts was carved into the life-size semblance of a man-at-arms; coverlet, canopy and curtains were of what seemed to be a crimson faced cloth, very fine to look at and clearly of a great weight; all the stuffs and hangings with which the furniture was done were of the same dignity. The floor was of polished oak.

We stole across to the door in the farther wall.

This admitted us to the royal dining-room.

This chamber resembled the Closet and was of much the same size. A handsome table stood in the midst of the floor.

We wasted no time but passed on.

A moment later we stood in the antechamber.

This was small, but notable. The walls were not panelled, but covered with tapestry. Two massive, high-backed chairs were all the furniture.

The door we now found before us was not at all like those through which we had come. It admitted of course to the gallery which led to the tower; and it was like a church door, that is to say, iron-studded, and Gothic in shape. A wrought-iron lock of great size was fixed upon the inside, and above this a simple latch which had only to be lifted to be freed.

If hope could but open gates, I think this door would have crumbled before our eyes; but hope cannot open gates, and—the door was fast.

Mansel stood very still.

At length he gave a short sigh and touched me upon the arm. A moment later we were moving the way we had come.

When we were again in the Closet, he put his mouth to my ear.

"Take a message to Hanbury. He and Carson will bring every tool we have to the south-west tower; then they will let fall a rope to the window of the ante-chamber, moving it to and fro until we take hold; when we do that they will come and take up the ropes which are hanging outside this room."

When I returned, Mansel was down on his knees by a hole in the floor. On the carpet, now drawn to one side, lay a square of polished wood. The recess which he had disclosed was floored by a grey, stone slab; this had a ring in its midst and was rudely locked into place by a pair of hasps and staples, the pins of which Mansel had withdrawn.

Gently I lifted the slab, to disclose the winding stair which led to the archway below.

"Can you hold it?" breathed Mansel.

I nodded.

At once he replaced the square of polished wood; then he laid the carpet, face downward, between my legs.

I lowered the slab.

Using the carpet as a sledge, we drew the slab into the Bedchamber and up to the King's bed. There we transferred it to my coat, and, lifting the crimson valence, thrust it beneath the bedstead and out of sight.

To restore the carpet to its place, close the window and take the wedge from the door took but a moment of time.

Then Mansel gave me a cloth and bade me polish the woodwork where we had stepped, especially about the casement which we had used.

When I had done so, he overlooked all with the torch.

Then we stole out of the room and closed the door.

Five minutes later we stood again in the antecham-ber and when we had opened a casement and found the rope, there was nothing to show, much less to sug-gest that we had seen the inside of any other room.

"And now the tools," said Mansel, "and then Hanbury. Carson to stay where he is. We shall make the devil's own noise, and he is to shoot at sight." I climbed up and gave the message as fast as I could.

The time was now half past three; the stars were no more to be seen, and rain had begun to fall. This was to our liking, for now any footprints we had made above or below would be wiped out; but the wet was against our foothold, and, as I came back, I slipped on the window-sill.

We had received the tools and were awaiting Hanbury, when some door within the castle was sharply closed.

It was some door behind us—not very far away.

Called upon to say which, I would have named the door of the Closet. The clash of a heavy, spring lock was unmistakable.

Mansel put out the light, and we stood as still as death, straining our ears for footsteps and hearing none.

A rustle without the window told us that Hanbury had begun to descend the rope.

We could not stop him for we had no signal-cord, and together we stood to the window to take him in without sound.

As we did so, came the creak of a floorboard, faint yet distinct. I would have said that it came from the Dining-room.

It was now as dark as pitch. I could not even see Mansel, two feet from where I stood.

Something swayed at the window....

Then we had George in our arms and Mansel was unfastening the rope which was holding him up.

Again I heard a board creak—somewhere at hand.

With the greatest force we lowered George to his feet. As we did so, the daïs upon which we were standing tilted suddenly forward, and, with nothing to save us, the three of us crashed to the ground. As we fell, the massive step resumed its proper position with a deafening clap.

There had been nothing to show that the step was not fixed, and, indeed, it was so solid that I do not think it would have moved under ordinary use; but the weight of three men happening to fall upon its edge had, I suppose, been too much for its counterpoise.

For a moment we lay as we had fallen, straining our ears; then Mansel got to his feet and lighted the torch.

"You two all right?" he said.

We told him "yes."

"Then quick," says he, "for, by thunder, we've rung the bell."

With that, he set Hanbury to watch the Dining-room door and hold the torch, while I took the stoutest chisel and laid its edge where the lock met the wood of the door.

"You strike," said Mansel, taking it out of my hand.

I picked up and swung a hammer with all my might....

I cannot attempt to tell the noise we made.

Perhaps our reluctance to make any noise at all and the infinite care we had taken to smother all sound magnified for us this sudden breach of silence; certainly the hour, the emptiness of the apartments and the style and proportions of the building made so many sounding-boards. Be that as it may, had the castle been full of troops and these been suddenly summoned by trumpet and tuck of drum I do not think the uproar could have won to our ears.

It took us, I suppose, two minutes to reduce that lock.

As Mansel wrenched it away, an iron fillet, into which its tongues were protruding, came also. This fillet was a false jamb, that ran the whole length of the door and was laid upon stone. Now that it was displaced, we could see that the door was bolted, top and bottom, upon the opposite side. The bolts were shot into the stone, but, the fillet gone, we could reach them and, with the slightest manipulation, could draw them clear of their sockets and open the door.

I put up a hand, but Mansel caught my arm. *Someone was pounding upon the other side of the door.*

Together we stared at the oak.

Then came Adèle's clear voice.

"Is that you, Jonah?"

"Yes, dear," said Mansel. "One moment, and—"

"No, no," cried Adèle. "Stop. Stay where you are. Rose Noble's here by my side. And he says if you open that door you'll lose your match."

6

The Love of a Lady

Never, I suppose were hopes lifted so high one moment and dashed so low the next.

Indeed, I was so much confounded by the sudden overthrow of our fortune that I stood staring at the door, as a clown at a strange fish, and when I turned to Hanbury, who had come across to our side, he was wearing the blank expression of a player of chess who, having but two moves to make to win his match, suddenly perceives that his opponent has but one.

And this shows how fine was the stuff of which Mansel was made, for, though our dismay was nothing to the bitterness which must have been his, beyond raising his eyebrows he gave no manner of sign that he was put out, and, what was far more, he had a plan in an instant to save the game.

Before he could answer Adèle, we heard the clatter of footsteps and, then, Rose Noble's deep voice speaking Casemate and Bunch by name.

Under cover of this distraction, Mansel caught us each by an arm.

"Time to be gone," he whispered. "We've shot our bolt. Leave everything and clear out. *I'm going to stay.* Food and dry clothes to me by the waterfall cord. And paper and pencil. So long."

Before we could speak, he had returned to the door.

"My dear Adèle," he said, "I'm delighted to hear your voice."

"Same here," said Adèle, cheerfully.

Rose Noble laughed.

"'Journeys end in lovers meeting,'" he said.

"How's Boy?" said Adèle.

"None too bad," said Mansel. "A bit hot and bothered you know, till we'd run you to earth; but that was natural. His leg's just splendid."

"How much does he know?" said Rose Noble.

That was as much as I heard, for Hanbury was at the window, and I had something to say before he was gone.

"I stay with Mansel," I said. "Give me your pistol and torch."

"I can't leave you here," said George.

"Quick," said I. "We'll argue another time."

With that, I put my hands in his pockets and helped myself. There was a bunch of wedges we had not used. These I took, and his torch. He gave me his pistol unwillingly enough. Then he shook his head and went up the rope.

High words were flying as I swung myself into the rain. Rose Noble was clearly angry, and I heard Adèle's scornful laugh....

As soon as my feet touched the terrace, I made my way to the water and scrambled under the door. I had a vile wet passage, but I managed to save both pistols and Hanbury's torch. The archway was dank and draughty, so I lost no time in finding the little staircase that served the trap-door and, when I had found it, in climbing as high as I could. Here I was out of the wind and might have been snug; but my clothes were wringing wet and that made the stone seem cold.

I was quite sure that this was the spot at which Mansel proposed to lie hid—for that, of course, was his plan. He intended Rose Noble to think that he had withdrawn, and, presently taking the monster off his guard, to strike again.

And here I may say that I found his plan very good. To release Adèle might be beyond our power, but our luck would be out indeed, if we could not kill Rose Noble before two days were gone by, and his death, as I have said, would break the enemy's back.

What Mansel would say, when he found me, I could not tell. He did not like disobedience; but for one man to stay alone in such an enemy's camp seemed to me out of reason, and I hoped very much that he would share my view.

I had not long to wait.

A sudden quickening of the rustle the water made told me that Mansel was passing beneath the door, and an instant later I heard his foot on the stair.

"Mansel," I breathed. "Chandos speaking."

"Ah, William," said he; and that was all.

He sat down on the step below mine and put his head in his hands.

After a little he spoke.

"I didn't dare stay. Rose Noble was bound to exploit a chance like that. You see, without an audience there's no point in doing her harm; but with me, so to speak, looking on.... He struck her, Chandos. And, because she wouldn't cry out, he struck her again.... And so it seemed best to go.... Oh, my God," he cried suddenly, "there are times when I'd take your offer and buy her out."

"It's always open," I said.

"I know," he said, "I know."

For a long time we sat in silence. Then he gave a short sigh.

"Drink some of this," he whispered, and put a flask into my hand.

It was brandy and did us both good, for our state of mind and of body was wretched enough.

Presently he spoke again.

"No," he said. "No. What's the good of buying a broken heart? We've got to beat Rose Noble; there's no other way. But it's a dreadful business to have to go so slow."

That was a true saying.

Indeed, the next sixteen hours were the worst I have ever spent. I can never remember them without a shudder, and to our restless senses they seemed more like sixteen days. Without cause we dared not emerge; no cause presented itself. The rain fell down without ceasing, and, though we took it in turns to watch from the archway, no one appeared in the courtyard, or, so far as I know, visited the terrace upon the opposite side. Command the terrace we could not, unless we lay down in the channel below the door; and that was dangerous, for the noise which the water made embarrassed the ear, and we might well have been noticed before we had time to withdraw. There was, however, the keyhole of the great door itself, and, whilst we were listening there, I do not think one could have passed without our hearing his steps.

We saw the dawn come in and the day draw to its close; we heard the drip of the rain and the sigh of the wind; and that was all.

One thing only we decided, for you cannot make bricks without straw, and we had no data with which to make any plan. We determined that, when night had fallen and we dared pull up the rope, we would enter the King's Closet and eat and rest in such comfort as that room could give. The risk of discovery was small, and, if we could not take shelter which would allow us to sleep, we should, we knew, be unfitted to strike when the moment came. I do not mean that when the day was over we had no resistance left, for we were both very strong and had suffered adversity far more exacting than this; but we knew that to rob Rose Noble the eye must be clear, the hand unearthly swift and all the senses at the very top of their pitch or, as the saying is, a man might as well go home.

At last the daylight faded, and the rain ceased.

When it was quite dark, we laid hold of the rope in the channel and took the strain. To our delight it was loaded, so, bidding me stay where I was and haul it in, Mansel crawled under the door and made for the balustrade beneath which the waterfall leapt.

At last I felt a check, and, very soon after, a package done up in oiled silk was thrust under the door.

Two minutes later we were in the King's closet, with good, oak boards beneath us and wedges under the doors.

As well as changes of clothing, Hanbury had sent us a blanket sewn into the shape of a bag; this was just what we needed and, with the square of carpet, promised a good night's rest.

But first there was work to be done.

There was food enough for five, and, what was better still, a bottle of excellent brandy by way of drink.

We changed and made our meal by the shaded light of a torch, for to do such things in the dark without making a sound required more time and care than we were prepared to expend; and, when we had done, Mansel wrote out the first message which we were to send to George:

George.

Send up Adèle's dressing-case.

(a) Is there any reason why we should not descend by this rope at any time?

(b) Where is the cover nearest to the foot of the cliff and what shape does it take?

I wished to go out this time, but Mansel would not consent. Whilst, therefore, I let down the message, he changed again into his dripping clothes, and, as soon as I took the strain, he returned to the balustrade....

Hanbury's answer was clear.

(a) No reason at all. We have lengthened the rope, so that it reaches the ground. By day the last forty feet will be concealed in a bush. No one could ever climb up without help from above.

(b) Beechwoods two furlongs north-east. Unless you direct otherwise, one car will be always concealed within sound of the drive, and one at the foot of this cliff from nightfall till dawn.

As soon as he had changed, Mansel wrote out his reply.

Good. Visit the beechwoods twice daily at ten and three. Don't wait any longer to-night. Send Carson and another to Poganec with the enclosed note instead.

The note was addressed to Captain Pleydell and was very short.

I have spoken with Adèle. She is very cheerful and seems to be in excellent health.

These dispatches I sent alone, and, when they were gone, we finally closed the trap-door and getting into our blanket, lay down on the carpet to sleep.

Whether Mansel rested I know not, but I slept like the dead. The Closet was full of pale light when I awoke, and Mansel was at the window, with his eyes on the east.

It was ten o'clock in the morning, the weather was very fine, and I had my ear to the keyhole of the archway door, when I heard a footstep upon the terrace beyond.

As I turned to summon Mansel, I felt his hand on my arm.

"Casemate is with her," he said.

The next instant he was down in the channel and was peering under the door.

Slowly Adèle and her warder passed into and out of my view. Her hair had been rudely shorn to the shape of her head, and about her shoulders she wore a rag of a shawl.

Then I heard Casemate's voice.

"—— this sunshine," he said. "Don't you want a hat on your curls?"

"No," said Adèle.

"Well, I guess I do," said Casemate. "You carry on, an' move. You're not here to wave to Charlie; you're here for exercise. An' Rose is red-hot this morning, so I shouldn't tread on his toes."

With that, he left her.

"Pull up the rope," said Mansel; and, before I could think, he was gone.

I was taken so much by surprise that, though I did his bidding, I could hardly believe that our attempt at rescue was fairly begun. Casemate was seeking his hat; that, before he returned, we should be able to let down Adèle to safety seemed to me a chance in a thousand, while, if we were caught in the act, her life would be in great peril and our present enterprise wrecked. I found it unlike Mansel to take such a risk and was wondering whether for once his zeal had outrun his discretion, when Adèle's face appeared in the channel almost between my legs.

In a flash I had her under the arms, and had drawn her clear of the door and lifted her up. Mansel followed at once, and, whilst I worked like a madman to pull up the rope, he spoke to Adèle.

"If we can do it in time, we shall let you down the face of the cliff. The moment you're down, unfasten the rope and run for your life to the beechwoods that lie north-east." He pointed the direction with his arm. "Over there. George or Carson will be there with one of the Rolls. Tell them to drive you—"

He stopped there, and, after listening intently, caught my wrist.

"Let go the rope," he breathed. . . .

For a moment I could hear nothing. Then came Rose Noble's voice.

"Hat be damned. I said 'See that she moves.' By ———, that's clean enough talking. D'you think—"

And there, I suppose, he saw that Adèle was gone....

For a moment there was dead silence. Then came a rush of steps to the balustrade.

Adèle and Mansel and I stood still as death, while the rope fled steadily back the way it had come. That Rose Noble must now observe it seemed almost certain; *whether he would see that it was moving we could not tell.*

A sudden roar from the terrace made my heart stand still.

"By ——, she's gone," screeched Rose Noble. "Look at that —— cord."

"She's never had time," cried Casemate. "I only—"

"*Time?* howled Rose Noble. "*Time?* It's only your white-livered sort that wants time to break out of hell. Bunch! Punter!" he yelled. "Turn out the —— car. Go and help them, you ——. And if we don't take her at the foot of this blasted rock I'll twist your block off your body with my bare hands."

Before the threat was issued, Casemate was gone. I could hear him shouting for Bunch like a man possessed.

The rope was now back in the channel and lying as snug and as taut as though it had never been touched.

Mansel was speaking low.

"Sit down on the step, dear, and let me pull off your boots."

Adèle obeyed him at once. She was, of course, drenched to the skin.

"Now go up these stairs; they'll bring you into a room. Your dressing-case is there. Change your clothes as quickly as ever you can. The instant you're through, come back."

Here came voices from the courtyard, and almost at once I saw figures about the car. This was in the midst of the archway that ushered the castle gate and directly opposed to that beneath which we stood. The car was standing, as we were, in deep shadow, but the courtyard was full of light. It follows that I could not distinguish whose the figures might be but, after a little, I heard Rose Noble's voice. I suppose the car was unready for her engine would not start for all the frenzy with which someone was swinging the shaft. Another—Casemate, I think—was clumsily dashing spirit into the tank....

At last with a stammer and then with a sudden roar the engine came to life; and that put an end to my observation, for the noise was deafening and a dense smoke from the exhaust screened any movement that was made.

Suddenly the gate was opened, and the car shot out. Mansel's hand touched my shoulder.

"Can you see who's shutting the gate?"

"I think it's the woman," said I. "Yes, I can see her skirt."

"Good," said Mansel. "And now I think we'll follow. But I hope the others won't try to get in their way. Could you tell at all how many got into the car?"

I shook my head.

"Rose Noble?"

"I assume so," said I. "I certainly heard his voice. Besides, you heard what he said."

"I don't count what he says," said Mansel. "If he saw that rope was moving, I've played my cards wrong."

"What else could you have done?"

"Followed Casemate and met him," said Mansel.

"But you couldn't have known—"

Mansel smiled.

"You never do—at cards," he said.

Adèle's voice came from the stairway.

"I'm ready, Jonah," she said.

A moment later we were in the King's Closet.

With the utmost caution Mansel opened the door; then he signed to Adèle to follow. I caught up her dressing-case and brought up the rear.

The King's Bedchamber was empty.

Like thieves in the night, we stole across its floor and into the Dining-room.

A moment later we entered the antechamber.

The door was as we had left it; but the hammers and chisels were gone, and the window was shut.

With a little manipulation I had the upper bolt free and wheedled it clear of the jamb. The lower, however, resisted, and Mansel, who was down on his knees, was able neither to turn it nor thrust it back.

At length he rose to his feet.

"Are the ropes there, Chandos?"

I stepped to the window, but the ropes were gone. When I told him, he frowned.

Then he wedged the door, so that it could not be opened from the opposite side, and rose to his feet.

"Come," he said, turning. "We must try the other end of the suite."

So we came back to the Closet and, passing through the Queen's rooms, entered the other antechamber which the bookseller's guide had shown us that we might expect.

There was now before us a door like that we had left, which gave, no doubt, into the other "gallery of stone."

And this door also was fast.

I confess that here the sweat ran over my face.

To be within hail of freedom, to have the prison to ourselves, to have come so far, only to be prevented, as rabbits left in a hutch, was almost more than I could bear.

Mansel took a wedge from his pocket and thrust it under the door. Then he led us back to the Closet and down the winding stair.

"Wait here," he said. "It's no good our all getting wet. I'm going through the door at the head of the terrace steps. That should be open, all right. And then, if I can, I'll draw that blasted bolt."

With that, he was gone.

I clapped my ear to the keyhole, and Adèle's hand stole into mine. I remember thinking that she was seeking comfort, but now I know that she would have comforted me. I was trembling so much that I could not keep my head steady against the wood.

Then I heard the sound which I dreaded, and trembled no more.

I heard Mansel go by with a rush, to try the opposite door.

He was back in an instant.

As I helped him out of the channel—

"I should have kept a chisel," he said. "But, chisel or no, we must try that bolt again."

Adèle laid a hand on his arm.

"You'll die of cold, dear," she said. "Have you dry things?"

"We mustn't wait, my lady. I—"

"I won't stir from here," said Adèle, "until you've changed."

Mansel smiled and was gone.

There were dry clothes in the Closet, for Hanbury had had the foresight to send us two changes apiece.

Adèle had me by the coat.

"Oh, why did you stay?" she breathed. "If Rose Noble gets him, he'll break him by eighths of an inch. I never knew what hate was, till I heard that terrible man. And he's got it in for Jonah from bottom to top. I'm nothing—a lever at most ... one of the levers of the rack. It's only the money that can save him. Remember that. Dying men can't sign cheques. But if ever the cheque is signed.... How much is he asking?"

"Five hundred thousand," said I.

I felt her fingers tighten upon my coat.

"He'd take a hundred thousand—*with Jonah thrown in*. I've heard him say so—not once, but fifty times. I tell you—"

"Chandos," said Mansel from the stairway, "pull in that rope. Cut a length of a hundred yards. If we can't shift that bolt..."

What else he said I never knew, for the moment I handled the cord, *I knew that it had been severed a few feet away.*

I think I must have exclaimed, for Mansel called sharply to know what the matter might be.

"It's cut already," said I, and, with that, I pulled in what was left and proved my words.

With his back to Adèle, Mansel looked me full in the eyes.

"I was right—just now," he said quietly. "I ought to have led out Clubs." Then he turned to Adèle. "Come, my lady," he said, "and we'll have another whack at that door."

"Tell me, Jonah," said Adèle.

"My dear," said Mansel, "Rose Noble's a careful man. He locks the door before the horse is stolen, but he takes the precaution of locking it afterwards, too. Never mind. We'll get out somehow."

When we entered the Closet, he picked up the bottle of brandy and poured some into a glass.

"The stirrup cup," he said, smiling, and gave the glass to Adèle.

Then he and I drank quickly.

A moment later we were crossing the Bedchamber's floor.

As we entered the Dining-room—

"That'll do," said Rose Noble.

There was nothing to be said or done.

The fellow was sitting in a chair at the head of the table, with his elbows upon the board and a pistol in either hand.

Never before or since have I felt so far out of my depth.

A moment before, we had had the suite to ourselves; the entrance doors had been wedged and as good as barred; no sound of any sort had come to our vigilant ears. Yet our movements had been closely observed, our intentions had been accurately gauged, and our enemy had been able to snare us with the effortless ease of a nurse outwitting a child.

"Keep your hands up," said Rose Noble, "and come and sit down—you two twopenny squirts to right and left, and the goods facing me. Move."

Slowly we did as he said.

"Now put your palms on the table."

Again we obeyed.

"And if anyone wants to die, they've only to move a hand."

Desperately I tried to marshal my wits, for if ever a clear head was needed to save the game, it was needed now; but my brain was ever wayward, and I remember thinking how strange a picture we made and how much astonished King Maximillian would have been, could he have viewed such a company gracing his private board.

Before me Mansel sat easily, leaning back in his chair. His hair was wet and rumpled, and he wore no collar or tie. His light, tweed coat, turned up about his neck, became him admirably and a quiet smile was lighting his handsome face. On my left Adèle sat upright; her colour was high and, because of her short, crisp hair, she looked like some old picture of a beautiful boy. She was wearing a fawn-coloured dress, and white silk was edging her delicate wrists and throat. Laid upon the smooth, dark oak, her lovely hands were unforgettable. And on my right, deep in the King's great chair, sat Rose Noble. One pistol lay before him; the other was in his right hand. His great bulk was loose as ever, and his huge face grey and flabby as when I had seen him first. He stayed so still that he might have been some gross idol, carved out of stone. Their lids, as usual, were almost hiding his eyes, and a faint smile was hanging upon the cruellest mouth that I have ever seen.

For a long time he held his peace, but at length he gave a smooth laugh.

"'Stone walls do not a prison make,'" he said softly. "An' I guess you three could heckle the guy that wrote that."

"My favourite maxim," said Mansel pleasantly. He looked across the table at me. "William," he said, "we must do better next time. There's a door behind our host—in the panelling. There's probably one in each room. They open into a passage which—"

"Quite so," drawled Rose Noble. "Quite so. I call it 'The Listening Post.'" His eyelids flickered, and the blood came into my face. "And now, perhaps, you'll let the geography stew and listen to me. I wasn't at Oxford College, but I guess the notes I've sent you were plain enough."

"As plain as my replies," said Mansel.

"I didn't hear them," said Rose Noble. "But, now we're so snug, maybe you'll say them again."

"The first thing," said Mansel at once, "Is to clear the air. This lady may be your prisoner, but I am not. One doesn't imprison one's broker if one happens to

116

want some funds. I mean, that's elementary."

"Maybe it is," said Rose Noble. "One don't spoil his right hand either. But I've known a guy that kicked when he had two lights, as mild as his mother's milk and when he had but one."

"I daresay you have," said Mansel. "It takes some people that way."

Rose Noble moistened his lips.

"I'm not out to break you," he said. "It's the goods that'll get the rough."

"Are getting the rough," said Mansel. "And there again I advise you to watch your step. 'Perishable goods' have a market; but 'damaged goods' make a very different price."

"They're not damaged—yet," said Rose Noble. "And I'm still waiting for a bid."

Mansel raised his eyebrows.

"A few months ago," he said quietly, "you stole some papers of mine. Give me them back, and I'll pay you a hundred pounds and hold my tongue."

I was aghast at this boldness and fully expected a truly dreadful outburst by way of reply. But none came; and after a little silence I breathed again.

Rose Noble lifted his lids and looked at Adèle.

I cannot describe the awfulness of his gaze. Hatred, malice and all uncharitableness burned in those terrible orbs. Themselves monstrous, their message was like unto them, and before its beastly menace my blood ran cold.

"You hear?" he said grimly. "You're pretty enough to fool round, but, when it's a question of paying, your gentleman-friend gets off."

Adèle flushed under his tongue.

"It's never been a question of paying," she said.

"Big words," said Rose Noble. "But they won't pull

you out of this mess. Your health and your name's on the counter; and if you fancy either, you'd better trouble Big Willie to open his purse."

"My name?" said Adèle, frowning.

"Your name," said Rose Noble softly. "You see, I'm not selling to your husband. I'm selling to the man next door."

Adèle's colour came and went. She looked round swiftly.

Then—

"You mean—"

"That I have not asked your husband to buy you back. That I have ignored his existence from first to last. That he's all sure and grateful that Big Willie's hoeing his row. *That Big Willie daren't undeceive him ...daren't so much as breathe my name—for fear of its putting ideas into his innocent head.*"

The brutal accuracy of this saying was to me like a buffet which makes the head sing again; and my brain seemed suddenly pygmy beside that of this terrible man.

Adèle had gone very pale.

"You mistake us," she said coldly. "Our understanding—"

"So I guess," said Rose Noble, as though she had not opened her mouth, "your pretty name is as much for sale as your health. Of course, if it isn't bought in, your husband can have it back. But it's not every fool, by ———, that'll pick up a rotten rose."

"I agree," said Mansel. "In fact, all you say would be very much to the point, if I hadn't told Captain Pleydell that I was in love with his wife."

Very slowly the blood flowed into Adèle's sweet face. She did not look at Mansel, and her eyes, which were resting on Rose Noble, never moved. But, after a little,

I saw that their focus had changed and that, though she was looking before her, she did not see, because she was lost in thought.

Rose Noble gave a thick laugh.

"I see," he said smoothly. "And, of course, he couldn't kick you—because of his leg. Well, well . . . And if you think that chokes me, you're nursing the dirty end. I guess I've a sleeve full of trumps—but if you don't want to see them you know the way."

"I'm afraid you'll have to play them," said Mansel. "You see, we don't mind paying, but it wouldn't amuse the lady to know she'd been bought."

"That's right," said Adèle.

Rose Noble sat back in his chair.

"You mean she don't care to be mortgaged outside your arms?"

"I didn't say that," said Mansel.

"I'll take it as read. I don't move around on your dunghills, but I guess a woman's a woman whether she's warming her maid or selling fish. This man can bend her fingers, and that one can go to hell. 'With love from little Willie' don't happen to suit her book. Maybe it don't suit yours. And so, I'll help you out." He leaned suddenly forward. "Be here in this room yourself a week from to-day, with two hundred and fifty thousand in Bank of England notes, and I'll let the three of you go."

"Nothing doing," said Adèle swiftly.

"I am not prepared," said Mansel, "to continue to talk this over while Mrs. Pleydell sits there."

Rose Noble's eyes narrowed.

"If you don't like the rules," he drawled, "you—well needn't play. I've picked my words so far, but run me up and I'm not going to cramp my tongue. If you're bunched round my table, God didn't put you there.

You horned right into this parlour, and, if you don't like the eats, I guess you can swallow them whole."

"I repeat my request," said Mansel. "I decline to—"

"I don't fancy that verb," snapped Rose Noble, using a savage oath. "You may feel ugly, but I've the right end of the gun. And now try and get me, you ———. I'm running this ——— party from the soup to the pineapple's bush. If you wanted a Bible reading, you've come the wrong day of the week. We're talking business this morning. It mayn't smell as sweet as lipsalve, but, if I find your linen dirty, I reckon you made it foul."

"I repeat my request," said Mansel steadily.

Rose Noble sucked in his breath. Then he opened his blazing eyes.

"Then finish," he said, "you ———. You say you've told her husband you want his wife. I'll give you some more to tell him, next time you meet. So far she's lived alone in her private suite. Bedroom and bathroom adjoining, as tight as you please. Now we'll cut out the bathroom, sonny, and she'll share—"

"I decline to—"

With a roar Rose Noble flung forward, and Mansel's bare hands shot out. The left struck aside the pistol, as Rose Noble fired; the right hit the beast on his mouth and knocked him into his chair. But for this, he must have gone down before the weight of the blow, but the chair was massive and, though it rocked for a moment, it held him up.

The sudden support saved him.

As I snatched at the second pistol, he swept it off the board, but the movement disordered his aim, and his second bullet went wide.

"Into the bedroom," yelled Mansel, hurling an oaken footstool, with all his might.

As I hustled Adèle through the doorway, I heard a screech of pain and a third report. Then Mansel whipped into the room and I slammed the door.

"Quick! Wedge the doors," breathed Mansel.

Now that we suspected their presence, the doors in the panelling were easy to find, and, since they opened inwards, before thirty seconds had passed the Closet and Bedchamber had been secured.

As I drove the last wedge, Mansel leaned his back to the wall and covered his eyes.

"That chair," he said brokenly. "That chair. It's enough to break a man's heart. I'd not time to hit him square, but I never so much as dreamed that that damned chair wouldn't go. If it had..."

Adèle put her arms round his neck, drew down his head to hers and kissed his lips.

"My darling," she said quietly, "no man could have done so well."

"By God, that's true," I cried.

"Oh, Adèle," said Mansel simply, "I do love you so much."

Then his arms went about her, and she hid her face in his coat.

Sitting on the floor of the Closet, I summed up our circumstances as best I could.

For the moment, Adèle was safe. What remained of the food which we had drawn up the cliff would last us with care for two days. We had three pistols, each holding seven rounds, and we had the run of two rooms and a way down into the archway—for what it was worth. That we could hold this position I had no doubt; indeed, it seemed most unlikely that Rose Noble would make an attack, for, unless we three could break out or Hanbury and the servants could break in, we must in three or four days fall into his hands.

For us to break out would be extremely hard; we had long ago perceived that the two "galleries of stone" were the keys to the royal suite, and that these were joined by a passage meant that we were surrounded by a guard-room which two men could hold against twenty, the inside of which we had not so much as seen.

With Hanbury and the servants we were no longer in touch. Our line of communication had been cut, and, even though George should decide to attempt our relief, I could not see that four men could bring this about. Six had been none too many two nights ago, and for four to repeat an assault which had only succeeded because it was a surprise seemed to me a hopeless adventure.

I found it hard not to believe that Fortune had taken her stand on the enemy's side. Had we known of the doors in the panelling, not once but five times over should we have won our match; without that precious knowledge, two nights ago we had all but rescued Adèle; if Rose Noble had not met Casemate in search of his hat, Adèle by now might well have been thirty miles off; but for the weight of the chair, Rose Nobel must have been dead ten minutes ago. This last was a bitter thought. Looking back, I perceived how Mansel had made the brute angry in order to make him move and had actually lured the master into the way of a fool, how he had ignored gross insult and let Adèle suffer in silence to gain his end, and how only the fear of depriving Adèle of his service had made him break off a battle which he might well have won.

Then I fell to considering Mansel and Adèle and their love—for now I was sure that she loved him as he did her—and what ever would be the outcome of an affair at once so passionate and so much out of joint.

God knows I did not blame them; I was rather exulting to see two such great hearts at one. It was the future that troubled me, the reckoning that would have to be paid.

And whilst I was in the midst of this reflection, the two came into the Closet, with shining eyes.

I got to my feet, and Adèle gave me her hand.

I kissed it naturally.

"William," she said, "I think I have the finest lover in the world."

"You have, indeed," said I, gravely.

"William the Faithful," said Mansel and laughed like a boy. He stepped to the trap. "And now," said he, "I'm going to spy out the land. Don't talk too loud, you two, and stay in the doorway, please, so that you can watch both rooms."

"Very good," said I, and went to my post at once.

When Mansel was gone, Adèle came to my side.

"Sit down, William," she said. "I want you to know how I feel."

We sat down on the floor, like two children, and Adèle leaned her head against the wall and slid her slight arm through mine.

"I'm in love with Jonah," she said. "I think I've loved him for years, but I never knew. And then, when I first saw Rose Noble and Jute pulled me off the mare, I remembered our talk in the forest and I knew what they wanted me for. They meant to hurt Jonah through me. That meant that Jonah loved me; and then, all of a sudden, I knew that I loved him. I was terribly worried at first, because it seemed so awful to be in love with anyone other than Boy. And then I came to see that, so long as nobody knew, no harm would be done. And I made up my mind that no one should ever know— not even Jonah himself . . . Well, you saw me break down.

You saw me kiss him and put my arms round his neck. I suppose I shouldn't have done it, but I'm so thankful I did. I want you to know that, William. And Jonah's so happy, too. We've had it all out and we both of us feel the same. You see, we're locked up here, in a sort of No Man's Land that lies between life and death. If we die—well, that's the end. If we live, then we go back. But we can't tell which it will be, and, so long as we're in that land, we're going to love each other with all our heart."

"But, oh, Adèle," said I, "what about going back?"

A very soft light came into her wonderful eyes.

"You can't take away memory," she said. "That we shall have forever, like a star that's always in the sky. I'm not seeking to justify myself. I know I'm another man's wife. But I don't care, William. Nature and Fortune have driven us into this Eden, and I don't think we should be human if we didn't help each other to pick the flowers."

"I don't think you would," said I heartily.

And that is the point of view I hold to-day. I daresay it cannot be defended. I can only say that Jonathan Mansel and Adèle were two of a kind that I never saw before and have never seen since. They were wise; "they were lovely and pleasant in their lives"; they were nonpareil; and, looking back, I find it most natural that, suddenly faced with life in the midst of death, two natures so alike and so peerless should have comforted each other.

Adèle looked at me swiftly.

"Do you mean that you understand? I don't think you can do that?"

"I can understand enough," said I, "to be very glad you're so happy."

"Thank you, William," she said. "And please don't

feel left out. Jonah was only saying a moment ago that you were the only living being he didn't mind seeing our love."

"History repeats itself," said I, indicating the rooms. "The equerry doesn't feel left by his king and his queen."

"Oh, he's a courtier," cried Adèle, clapping her hands.

"Don't slander my lieutenant," said Mansel, putting his head through the floor. "And here's a piece of good news." He sank his voice to a murmur. "The car is still out."

"Which means?" breathed Adèle.

"I hope and believe it means that it's gone for good, that George and the servants have got it and all or some of its crew. When Rose Noble sent them out, he knew very well that there was nothing to see; he knew we were in the archway and he sent them packing to mislead us and draw us out; I admit he pulled that off, but, unless and until they return, I believe he's alone."

I suppose that I showed my excitement, for he continued at once.

"But please remember Rose Noble's a host in himself. He may be single-handed, but he's worth ten ordinary men. And so we must watch and wait. If only we'd known of that passage two nights ago—"

"Then," said Adèle, "you'd never have known that I loved you. And now, please, I'm hungry. Will one of you give me some food?"

Mansel smiled.

"Feminine influence, William, is a terrible thing. With this girl-child round our necks, we shall forget we're at war."

"Forget it," said I, rising, "for half an hour. While you two lunch, I'll watch the castle gate."

"Very well," said Mansel, hoisting himself to the floor.

"But keep in the shadow and report the first sign of life. If Hanbury's sunk the pinnace, I don't think what's left of her crew will come aboard before dark. At least, they'll be fools if they try. But we can't hang our lives on guess-work and so we must watch. And, by the time I've eaten, I may have some plan."

But he had not; neither had I.

Through all that afternoon we three might have been alone in the Castle of Gath. If others spoke or moved, we neither saw nor heard them, and, when the light faded, we were still without any grounds on which to base any belief.

Of the ways of the castle Adèle knew far less than we, for she had been brought in blindfold and had never, before we seized her, been beyond the "gallery of stone"; but, had she been able to tell us that a tunnel led out of the chapel to Salzburg itself, the knowledge would not have helped us, for we dare not use the passage, in case it was held.

What remained of the waterfall cord was some sixty feet long, and this we had all ready to help our escape. Could we, therefore, have gained the roof, we could doubtless have reached the spur; but we had no means of ascent, and, though I essayed both chimneys, these were built of hewn stone and only a very small child could have made it sway up their shafts.

But for Adèle, Mansel and I would have sallied and might well, I think, have escaped. If the passage was under fire, at least it must be lighted by windows which overlooked the courtyard, and we would have chanced a lot in order to reach the gate. To such a risk, however, we dared not expose Adèle. Here I think we were wise. Unless he could starve us to surrender, Rose Noble's hope of ransom was gone by the board; once we sallied, therefore, the fellow had nothing to gain by sparing our lives—but much to lose, for he knew very well that we would shoot him at sight. Add to this that we had lately enraged him as never before, and you will see that to run such a gauntlet, with Adèle, so to speak, in our arms, was out of the question.

At last we decided to write a message to George and making it into a parcel, to cast it over the cliff.

So far as my memory serves me, this was how the note ran:

George.

The rope has been cut. We are fast in the Closet and the Bedchamber and we have got Adèle. There is a passage connecting the two stone galleries and looking upon the courtyard. You will attack to-morrow—Friday, half an hour after dark. As before, gain the roof; go directly to the door in the south-west tower; guard that; then let fall three ropes to the windows of the King's Closet; the moment these are in place, demonstrate. You will demonstrate by letting down a ladder to one of the windows of the passage and accidentally breaking the glass. Carefully rehearse the demonstration, which must last one minute. Whilst it is going on, you will take up Adèle by one of the ropes; rush her along the roof, lower her down to the spur and run with her for the wood; Chandos and I will follow. Not counting the caretakers, Rose Noble is, I think, alone—except for those who escaped when you stopped the car. Work out the whole attack with the greatest care; it must not fail.

We wrapped the note in oiled silk and then in a wet coat of mine, to serve as ballast; this we made into a parcel, and at ten o'clock that night I hurled it over the cliff.

Neither Mansel nor I had expected to sleep at all, for the castle gate had to be watched as well as the doors of the chambers in which we lay; but Adèle insisted on taking her turn with us, so each of us slept for two hours and watched for four.

Adèle was the first to rest, and I was the last; and I remember how I stole up the stairway at two o'clock, to find the rooms full of moonlight., Adèle in the midst of the doorway with her fair head against the jamb, and Mansel sleeping like a child, with her arms about him and his head in her lap. And, when he was gone to the archway and I would have lain alone, she would not have it so, but made mè lie down as he had and pillow my head upon her.

The castle gate was not opened during the night, and this made us certain that those that had left with the car were in Hanbury's hands.

We, therefore, decided to watch no more from the archway, but only to use it as and when we required. To this end we stopped the keyholes of the door and the gate and wedged a cage-grate in the channel beneath the door, to prevent an entry by stealth while our backs were turned.

And here let me say that before it was light we had all three bathed in the channel and made as fair a toilet as our means would allow. Mansel and I could do no more than shave and make ourselves clean, but Adèle must change her frock for one of a powder blue, and, when we sat down to breakfast, she was as point-device in appearance as though she had just left her bedroom in London Town.

The day passed quietly enough, and, except that one of us was always in the Bedchamber, listening for any sound, we kept no particular watch.

Adèle and Mansel were happy as the day was long.

I have never seen two beings so plainly glad of each other, so easy and natural in their love. There was nothing common or unclean in all their tenderness, and, so far from embarrassing my senses, my acquaintance with such devotion lifted up my heart.

One thing only troubled us, and that was the absolute silence which reigned without our doors.

That Rose Noble should make no sound was natural enough; yet the continuous absence of any sign of life came to insist that we had the castle to ourselves and to tempt us against all reason out of our lair. This temptation we certainly resisted, but with every hour the suggestion that we were alone increased in strength, until when the evening came, we were all three unsettled and did not know what to think. In a way this did not matter, for, if, indeed, Rose Noble were out of the way, our release by Hanbury must be a simple affair; yet the bare idea of such fortune seemed something sinister, like the counsel of a prophet whose eyes are not straight in his head.

"The truth is," said Mansel, "we ought to have played his game. We shouldn't have made a sound for twenty-four hours. Then he'd 've begun to wonder if we were gone; and at last he'd 've tried to find out and shown his hand. As it is, the positions are reversed, and he's fairly got us guessing—which is just what he wants."

This was uncommon sense, but, even whilst I agreed, I found myself supposing that Rose Noble was dead or gone and finding the supposition curiously untoward.

For this strange uncertainty of outlook I have never been able to account; I am not given to imagining vain things, or to letting my fancy fly in the face of fact; yet, though I was not uneasy, my mind would not come to rest, but continually dwelled upon the silence and the prosperous tale which it told.

At last the day was over, and dusk came in.

When it was dark, we opened the Closet windows and shut the trap-door. Then Mansel set me at a window, with Adèle by my side, and himself to watch the Bedchamber until the moment should come.

The night was most black and still, and I stood leaning out into the thunderous air, straining my ears for the rustle of a rope coming down....

But none came; and, after a long time, I began to feel sick at heart.

I did not move, for the night was before us, and while it was dark we could hope; but Hanbury was always punctual—and now he was late....

I do not know how long I stood there, but suddenly my heart bounded as I heard a movement above.

An instant later I had a rope in my hands....

As I put my weight upon it, another rope brushed my arms, and almost at once, a third.

By my silent direction, Adèle gave one flash with her torch and, in a twinkling, Mansel was by our side.

Himself he tested the ropes; then he bound one about her and lifted her on to the sill.

Adèle put her arms round his neck and pressed her face against his.

So we stayed, waiting....

Then came a clatter from the passage the shiver of broken glass.

"My beautiful darling," said Mansel, and swung her out of the window and into the night.

For a second he watched her rising, then he drew back.

"You next, William," he said; "as quick as you can."

At once I leaned out to grope for the other two ropes.

"Quick," breathed Mansel. "That demonstration's too thin."

Desperately I flung out both arms, sweeping the air—
and found nothing.

"They're gone," I cried, drawing back. "They
were—"

Mansel was at the next window, leaning out and craning his neck.

As I did the same, a very faint exclamation came
down from above.

And then a thick laugh.

"Isn't that nice?" said Rose Noble.

7

We Practise to Deceive

Try as I will, I cannot distinctly remember what then
took place, and I think that I acted blindly, as a man
in a trance.

I know that we were both in the passage, the main
doors of which were fast shut, that our rope was dangling from a window and that Mansel was about to go
down, when the beam of a torch illumined his head
and shoulders, and a bullet sang past his ear.

I know that the light and the shot both came from
directly above, so that, placed as we were, we could
not so much as reply.

I know that we were both on the terrace and that
Mansel was casting the rope in the vain hope of catching a merlon in the noose he had made.

I know that we were both in the antechamber, that
the great door was as we had left it and that, whilst I

fought like a madman to shift the bolt, Mansel was kneeling beside me with his head in his hands....

At last I felt a touch on my shoulder, and Mansel got to his feet. I followed him into the Dining-room slowly enough. My head was strangely heavy, and I felt shaken and spent. Had he bade me lie down and sleep, I should have done his bidding without a word. The shock of what we had done had left me listless.

Mansel sat down in a chair, and I sat down in another and waited for him to speak.

To be honest, I hoped he would stay silent, for I could think of no comment upon our case which would not be bitter as death and wholly vain; but, when he began to speak, he did so with such composure as fairly shamed me out of a humour so recreant and so mean.

"Something, of course," he said quietly, "has happened to George. I can tell you the time when it happened—ten o'clock yesterday night. He was awaiting a message at the foot of the cliff. No doubt he was being watched. And, when the packet fell down, the enemy laid him out and picked it up. When I say 'George,' I mean 'George and the servants,' of course. They're not four any more—four effectives; they may not even be three....

"Point number two—*Rose Noble is not alone*. He may have been yesterday morning, but he's certainly not alone now. I suppose he took them in by a rope some time last night. Anyway, he's smarter than I am, and Punter or Casemate has certainly bested George.

"Point number three—*we must get out of this suite*. I should never have split our force; and now, by hook or by crook, I've got to join it again. If Carson or George is alive, they'll attack to-night, and we've got to open the gate and let them in. What's a thousand times worse, if we're still at his mercy to-morrow, Rose Noble will put on the screw...."

"Point number four—*the 'hands-up' phase is over.* From now on seeing is shooting, and shooting to kill. Rose Noble's still hoping to break me, for the sake of doing a deal; but he knows it's a chance in a million and he's not going to risk his life by sparing mine."

And there, I remember, he happened to cast down his eyes.

We were not without light, for he had the torch in his hand, but this he was holding downward, so that its beam made a circle upon the floor.

For a moment he did not move. Then he was out of his chair and down on his knees....

Clean around the table there was a crack in the floor.

It was a very fine cleft and was choked with dust and the wax with which the floor had been rubbed; but these gave way at once to the point of a knife, and then we could see that the floor had been sawn asunder with the finest of saws.

I could scarcely believe that here was another trap-door, for, for one thing only, the cleft was surrounding the table with a fair two inches to spare, and a trap-door some eight feet by five seemed out of reason; yet, for some purpose or other, the floor had been cut, and, what seemed to me still more strange, except by the dust and the wax, the cleft had never been stopped.

Mansel was speaking in my ear.

"The table sinks through the floor. I saw it once before in some castle. The idea was to gain privacy. No servants in the room; but the table descended and rose between each course." He touched the smooth oak beneath the table. "This piece of the floor is really no more than a lift: and, if we can find out its trick...."

I sought to move the table, but it was fixed to the floor.

"That's right," breathed Mansel. "The other I saw was fixed. I remember they said it was raised by a system of pulleys and weights. The weights weighed far more than the table, so it couldn't descend on its own or so much as budge, but had to be hauled down by a windlass between each course."

"It's as firm as a rock," said I, stooping. "You don't think it's locked into place."

Mansel shrugged his shoulders.

"We must try to find out," he said. "If we can weight it enough...."

Then I saw that, with four counterweights, each, let us say, of the weight of the table and lift, these two would seem as much fixed as though they had beneath them a girder to hold them in place—, *until there was laid upon them a burden three times their own weight;* but that if we could manage to load them to this extent the table would sink through the floor and open a way of escape.

In silence we lifted the chairs and set them upon the board; they were immensely heavy, but the table stood fast. Ten more chairs we added, bringing them one by one from the other rooms and using our rope to lash the perilous pile. But, though we added our weight, the mass never budged.

And here we were brought to a standstill, for, though there were yet more chairs, we had used all the rope we had and we could not think how to get them on to the top of the structure their fellows made.

Suddenly I thought of the slab which Mansel and I had hidden beneath the King's bed....

We had dragged this into the chamber, and I was under the table, with my feet braced against the great stretcher, hauling the stone into place, and sitting, as it happened, directly upon the cleft, when I felt a definite movement beneath my seat.

At once I told Mansel, and, after a short consultation,

we lay down upon opposite sides and, taking hold of the stretcher, began to pass by inches on to the lift.

As I drew myself on, I felt this beginning to move, and all at once we were sinking into some cold, dark place.

We must have come down with a crash, but the chairs we had piled on the table were overlapping the lift, and, when these were prevented by the floor, the lift, thus relieved of their weight, immediately stopped.

The torch now showed us a cellar, with a door in its eastern wall. About us was the massive cage in which the lift ran, and at each of its corners were a pulley and a rope and a great counterweight of stone. A little to one side stood the windlass, as Mansel had said.

And now, once again, as they say, we had the wolf by the ears.

The floor was but eight feet away, but, if one of us was to descend, the lift would instantly rise and, taking the other up, lock him once more into the Dining-room; while, if both descended at once, the lift would shoot back into place with a shock which would shake the castle and send the twelve chairs crashing to wake the dead.

But, after a little reflection, Mansel found out a way.

On the under side of the lift, right in its middle, was a hook; to this was attached the great rope which the windlass controlled. If we could reach this rope, the trick was ours.

Mansel took my left wrist in his hands and lowered me clear of the lift. At once I swung to and fro until I could reach and lay hold of the great iron hook. With my left hand I then laid hold of the edge of the lift, and Mansel climbed round my body and seized the rope. Then we came down the rope together, on to the ground.

We let the lift rise by inches, until it was back in its place, and then, with one accord, we turned to the door.

This was unfastened and brought us directly into what seemed a great hall.

For a moment I thought we were out, for I heard the gurgle of water as plain as could be, but then I perceived that the air was the air of a crypt, dank and something musty and very still.

After listening carefully, we ventured to light the torch.

The place was a kitchen, but had not been used as such for a number of years. There was the huge fireplace, with the chains for the spits hanging down, and a grate like a hay-rack to serve a dozen joints. Five great, shuttered windows were looking upon the courtyard, and a doorway, whose step was muddy, was in the same wall.

And on the hearth lay George Hanbury, with his wrists and his ankles bound and a gag in his mouth.

That George had been left there to live, if he could, but, if he could not, to die we had not much doubt. He had lain there, gagged and bound, for twenty-four hours; his bonds had never been loosened, he had been given no water, much less any food; he had not so much as been visited. And such as will so use a prisoner are scarcely like to be troubled to find him dead.

Happily George was strong, and his condition of health as fine as ours, and, when we had set him free and had chafed his limbs, he was able to rise and to walk as straight as he pleased. It was clear, however, that he must have food and drink, and, since there remained in the Closet some brandy and bread and meat, we made our way back to the cellar without delay.

By using the windlass, we had the lift down at once, but, when I would have gone up, Mansel put me aside.

"I'm going," he said. "And please give me full five minutes before you bring me down. Now that one's got to go back, he may as well cover our tracks; the pile of chairs doesn't matter, but that slab would make anyone think."

With that, he mounted the lift, and I hoisted him up.

And while he was gone, George Hanbury told me his tale.

"When the car came out of the castle, I was down by the beechwoods at the foot of the cliff. Rowley was with me, but Carson and Bell and Tester were on guard, within sound of the drive.

"Carson heard the car coming, and the moment it passed he gave chase. I don't know whether they had expected this, but they did the best they could think of to shake him off. Of course they failed. They didn't bother much about the foot of the cliff; they certainly went that way, for I saw them go by, but they passed at sixty and never so much as slowed up. The sight of them worried me, but I didn't see what I could do but stay where I was. Of course Carson could have caught them, but, as Bell and he were alone, he thought he couldn't do better than cling to their heels. For half an hour they had the devil's own luck—never a check. Then comes a hairpin bend, and two hundred yards further on a flock of sheep....

"When Carson rounded the corner, Bunch was fifty yards off and *turning his car*. Sheep or no, it was an excellent move. The car has a shortish wheel-base, but a Rolls takes some getting round. Then Carson did well. He stopped, went into reverse and started to back to a turning he'd marked at the top of the hill. Before he could get there, Bunch was coming like hell. There was Punter beside him, and Casemate was back in the car. As they went by, Punter fired full at Carson and hit the brim of his hat...."

"This annoyed Carson and Bell, and I must say I'm not surprised. And, as soon as the Rolls was round, they put her along. By this time Bunch had stolen a bit of a start, but they gradually overhauled him, and, choosing a smooth bit of going, Bell took a shot at their tank. He didn't hit it that time, but he laid it open the next...."

"It was now a matter of time and nothing else. Bunch might do another three miles, but he couldn't do more, so Carson fell back a little, to keep, as he judged, out of range. Considering they'd fired again and made a hole in the screen, I think he was wise.

"They were now not more than six miles from the foot of the cliff, and heading that way. The road was full of bends, so half the time the cars were out of each other's sight. You can guess what happened. Three miles on Carson rounded a bend to see the car, doors open, by the side of the road. Of course, he put down his foot and went by a blue streak. Two shots were fired, but they didn't do any harm.

"Then Carson drove back to the spur, and he hadn't been there ten minutes when I came in. I was as pleased as Punch when I heard his report. I assumed they'd gone out to get food; and now their car was done in, and they were cut off. We fairly picketed that spur. A ferret couldn't have passed the line we held....

"Bell and I visited the beechwoods at three. I hated leaving the spur, but it didn't seem prudent for one to go out alone. We saw no one, and, when we got back, Carson had nothing to report.

"At last it began to grow dark, and I had to face two fresh facts. The first was this. According to plan, one of the cars must now leave for the foot of the cliff *and stay there perhaps till dawn*. That was awkward enough, but the second was worse. It was a yard of pearls to a bootlace that Punter and Casemate and Bunch would try to get home that night.

"After a lot of reflection, I decided to go alone to the foot of the cliff. I went. I meant to take Tester, but at the last I forgot. I found the rope gone and imagined you'd pulled it up. At ten o'clock something fell down about ten yards from where I stood. As I bent over it, somebody laid me out....

"Well, there you are.

"The next thing I knew I was lying in the back of the Rolls, which was doing forty over a wicked road. Then I was taken out and hauled through a ground-floor window into the Castle of Gath.

"Of course it was easy. When the servants heard the Rolls coming, they thought it was me. They probably thought it odd that I should drive on up to Gath, but, before they'd scented the trouble, the fat was burnt."

As I bent again to the windlass, my mind was full.

Not only was Rose Noble's foresight a fearsome thing, but the fellow was very well served. Punter and Bunch and Casemate had done uncommonly well. But what struck me most of all was that, though their car had been ruined and the Rolls was at their gate, the temptation to take her inside had been withstood. That for this resolution we had Rose Noble to thank, I have no doubt; the others would scarce have renounced so handsome a prize. Yet, had we seen the Rolls in the archway, the sight would have told us that George was out of the running, and Adèle would not have been delivered into the enemy's hand. This was the pink of strategy—the casting away of a sceptre to win a crown; and I must confess a sudden, craven fear that we should never outwit a man so firm of purpose and so unearthly wise.

The gurgle of water in the kitchen came from a little well. This had been sunk in the floor and was fed by a pipe which clearly ran out of the channel we knew so well. A similar pipe was conducting the overflow. By this simple device, the cooks had always fresh water ready to hand, and, what is more to the point, poor George was able to drink and to bathe his aching jaws. Then we plied him with brandy and made him eat what there was, for, though he made light of his bondage, a man cannot suffer as he had and feel as sound the same night.

While he was eating and drinking, we laid our plans.

That the servants were close at hand we had no doubt. Indeed, it seemed certain that they would any moment attack. If they did so before we could reach them, they would assuredly fail, for, for one thing only, they would enter by way of the roof, which the enemy was holding against our escape from the suite. They would thus walk clean into a trap, of which we, below, could not warn them, because we could not climb up. We, therefore, determined to make at once for the gate and, opening this if we could, to bring them in. If we could contrive to do this without being seen or heard, we should for the first time have the advantage of the enemy, for, whilst they were sure that they had but two men to deal with, and those under lock and key, in fact there would be six men free and within their camp.

The kitchen-door was unlocked and yielded without any fuss.

As we looked into the courtyard, hardly daring to breathe, the beam of a torch swept the wall beneath which we stood. It was little more than a flash and came, as before, from above; but it showed that the passage windows were still being watched. We had expected no less, but, although the beam was directed upon the wall, it lighted quite twenty feet of the courtyard itself, and, unless we could cross this belt between the flashes, we could not fail to be seen.

"No good waiting," breathed Mansel. "We must go across one by one. The first twenty feet on foot and as hard as we can; then, down on your face and crawl the rest of the way. If we go lightly, the water will cover our noise. Chandos first. Wait for me in the porch; I may be a little time coming, because I must shut this door. And now stand by."

Whilst he was speaking, the flashes came and went, but at intervals so irregular that no observation could help us, and we had nothing to do but to take our chance.

At last Mansel gave the word, and I made my dash.

As I fell on my face, a flicker lit up the courtyard....

Ten minutes later we were all three in the porch.

The wicket-gate was locked, and its key was gone. We, therefore, made ready to open the great gate itself, using the greatest care to make no sound. And here, to our vexation, we met with another check. Though we could feel the great bolts, we could not make out how to draw them, for each was engaged with some catch which we could not release. It was dreadful to stand there fumbling, because of some simple holdfast never devised to embarrass a porter's hand, but intended to prevent the bolts turning under battery of the gate. Yet show a light we dared not; and, as the minutes went by and the catch still mocked our fingers for want of sight, I began to feel that Fortune was not so much frowning upon us as laughing at us in her sleeve.

Then Mansel gave a short sigh and drew his bolt, and a moment later his fingers were playing with mine.

As the door yielded, he put his mouth to my ear.

"You go and find them," he said. "Hanbury and I stay here. If you don't strike them at once, try using the torch. But—"

And there, somewhere behind us, a shot rang out.

As we swung round—

"I saw the flash," said Hanbury. "*Up on the roof.*"

I ran full tilt into Rowley, who was standing at the foot of the ladders, with a cord in his hand.

"Oh, thank God, sir," says he. "We thought you were gone."

I shook him by the shoulder and pointed up to the roof.

"Recall them!" I cried. "Recall them! How can you get them back?"

He was tugging at the cord, like a madman, when another two shots rang out.

I could not stand there idle, but began to go up the wall.

I was on the second ladder, when someone above me looked down.

"Is that you, Bell?"

"Yes, sir."

"Get Carson and come down to the gate."

"Very good, sir."

I slid and fell back to the ground, to run to the gate. Mansel was standing, waiting, cool as a man in a garden, regarding his flowers.

"Carson must stay out," he said. "I daren't have everyone in. He and Tester must feed us and keep the cars. Send him for food and drink, as soon as he's down. And two fifty-foot lengths of rope. The others come in."

Whilst he was speaking, another four shots were fired,

and I ran back to Rowley with my heart in my mouth.

Him I sent to the gate and took his place. I think he was glad to go, for the firing was growing hotter, and to stand at the foot of the ladder in the knowledge that those you were awaiting might very well never come down pulled at a man's nerves.

Such concern will seem out of reason. When six men set out in a body to play with fire, it hardly becomes them to tremble lest someone be burned. But our outlook was not so simple. We feared no more for Carson than Carson feared for himself; but we all of us feared very much for the matter in hand. Our school was not that of Rose Noble. If one of us was wounded, we could not let him lie; he would have to be saved and attended at any cost; how high that cost would be no one could tell, but, placed as we were, we all knew that such a distraction might ruin our enterprise.

It seemed an age before Bell began to descend....

"Are you hit?" said I.

"Oh, no sir," said he. "Nor's Carson. But, of course, we had to go slow."

I sent him to Mansel at once.

Then a shot was fired right above me, and Carson came down with a run.

"Come," said I, and led him away up the spur....

It was well that I did so, for a light leaped out of the darkness, and a bullet went over our heads. To round the picture, I turned and fired back at the torch. No doubt the bullet went wide, but the light was put out.

Then I stopped and gave Carson his orders and told him that we were all safe, and he promised to be at the gate in a quarter of an hour. Then I stole back to the castle, and Mansel took me in.

Two doorways led out of the archway, one upon either hand. These Mansel set us to watch till Carson should come; "but I don't think," said he, "they'll disturb us; they've got their hands full. They've the roof to watch, and the passage, and it won't be light for three hours."

Here he was right, for Carson came and went, but nobody else; and, though lights flashed on the roof and the passage windows were closely and continually watched, no one came down to the archway or entered the great courtyard.

Carson went heavily away, for, though his part was most dangerous—because, except for Tester, he was alone—and though he would be the sole link between us and the world we knew, he had the true heart of a fighter and could hardly bear to leave us at such a pinch.

Early next morning he was to drive into Lass and there to take in supplies which should last us a week. He was then to bestow the two cars as best he could, somewhere beyond the wood and by the cross roads. He was not to move during the day, but by night he was to come to the spur and there wait till one of us met him or else it was dawn.

Then Mansel shut the gate and shot the great bolts and set his face again to the business of reaching Adèle, or, to be more precise, of thrusting between her and Rose Noble, *before the latter knew we were there.*

One thing was plain. Before the night was over, we must either have accomplished our purpose or have gained some room or corner where we could lie hid. Now the only shelter we knew was that of the cellar beneath the dining-room's floor, but, since our goal was as ever, the south-west tower, we decided to make for the latter and to trust to striking another and more convenient lair.

Now, though we knew next to nothing of the way

from the porch to Adèle, we had one valuable clue.

When Casemate had been hounded by Rose Noble to "turn out the car," he had certainly reached the porch as quickly as ever he could. Now his shortest path, as we knew from the bookseller's guide, was down the Grand Staircase and across the courtyard. *But Casemate had not crossed the courtyard.* It was, therefore, perfectly plain that that way was shut.

We, therefore, turned to the door in the western wall of the porch, for Casemate had come out of that, and that could, therefore, lead us back to the "gallery of stone."

I could set down our passage in detail, for I remember most clearly every step that we took. The hopes and fears which attended us, the sudden shocks of thankfulness and dismay, the waves of suspense and relief—all these are engraved upon my memory as letters cut upon a stone. But I think that such a recital would be out of place, for only those that were there could find it moving, and I have not the mind or the skill to trick it out.

And so I will only say that by galleries, stairs and chambers we made our way in the darkness towards the south-west tower. Again and again boards creaked beneath our weight, and sometimes, do what we would, a hinge would whine; we made mistakes in our going and were forced to retrace the steps we had been at such pains to take; and we went at a true snail's pace and as blind men go, for we dared not use our torches in case their light should betray us and ruin our game.

At break of day we stood in a little lobby that looked out upon the mountains and seemed at that misty moment to command the world.

The place had the look of a guard-room, and so, I am sure, it had served, for a wicket gave directly on to a winding stair, which if a man ascended he came to the roof, but, if he went down, *he came to the "gallery of stone."* It was, indeed, the stairway of the south-west tower.

So we broke and entered into that jealous keep which for six long days had mocked us and all our works.

The need for caution was now paramount.

We stood at the enemy's elbow, and he did not know we were there. We had our hand almost upon him; but he had his hand on Adèle. He was unready, but we did not know the ground. If we could strike before he could, the game was ours; but if we were to be behindhand, we had better be sitting at Lass with our hands in our lap.

We afterwards found that there were in the tower three apartments, consisting of two rooms each. These were a bedroom and bathroom, very well done. The window from which Adèle had signalled was that of the middle apartment, the door of which, as she had told us, gave into the "gallery of stone."

For a long time we crouched like animals, straining our ears; but we could hear no sound. Then Mansel breathed his orders, and we began to move....

George stood fast in the lobby, ready to shoot at sight; Bell and Rowley stole three steps up the stair and stayed with their backs to the wall and their knives in their hands; and Mansel, with me behind him, began to go down....

It was dark in the gallery, for all its five doors were shut, but a pale smear of light was betraying the threshold of the door which led to the terrace steps. That gave us our bearings at once, but, if there was someone there, we could not see him, and the silence all about us was that of death.

Then came a sigh of the wind, and something moved.

It was a door on our right—the door of the prisoner's room.

Very slowly we watched it open, letting the daylight out. I could see Mansel just before me, covering the gap with his pistol and steady as any rock. I could see beyond him and into the very room. The floor was bare and polished, and the walls were panelled with oak.

Then, very slowly, the door began to close.

In a flash Mansel had stopped it, and we were within the room.

This was empty.

A window had been left open, and that had occasioned the draught. The bathroom was empty, too. Adèle was gone.

Two minutes later we had proved the truth to the hilt.

The three apartments were vacant, and the door to the roof was shut. Rose Noble, prisoner and all had withdrawn to the opposite tower.

It was a bitter business.

That our labour was lost was nothing; but the waste of time shocked us, and the thought that, so far from progressing, *we were now twice as far from Adèle as we had been at the time when we stood in the porch* was plain torment.

That we never had any doubt where Rose Noble and his prisoner were gone, I attribute to Mansel alone. Only a brilliant perception can rip the skin off an assumption and bare a fact. Everything certainly argued withdrawal to the south-east tower; but that was not nearly enough. We had to *know*. And Mansel knew.

I have said we were now twice the distance that we had been from Adèle. And so it seemed, for we dared not use the roof during the day and, as we had reason to know, the way by the Royal Apartments was straitly barred. Yet the thought of returning to the porch and thence beginning again to grope our way was hardly to be endured, because the clock was against us and we feared to let go so much time. Cross the porch in daylight we could not, because of the man on the roof. We must, therefore, wait until nightfall to make the move—some sixteen hours of inaction, when time was so very dear. The harder we stared upon this prospect, the more ugly and hazardous it grew; the more the daylight broadened, the more perilous seemed delay. Any moment Rose Noble might discover that Mansel and I had escaped; any moment the kitchen might be entered, and Hanbury's release become known; any moment one of the gang might stumble into our arms, and, though we could stop his mouth, his failure to reappear would tell its tale. And if none of these things happened and we lay close until night, would our passage be so successful as the passage that we had made? *Was there a way within doors to the south-east tower?* And what of the caretakers? That we had not found them last night suggested most strongly that their rooms lay the other side; and if we encountered the woman, she was most sure to give tongue....

For an hour we stayed in the gallery, keeping such watch as we could and, for my part, feverishly considering what we should do.

At length Mansel bade us all listen and, with the plainest reluctance, unfolded the following plan.

"Mr. Chandos and I must re-enter the Royal suite. That we can do from this end without any fuss. Mr. Hanbury with Bell and Rowley will go to the top of this tower. Ten minutes after we have entered, Mr. Chandos will give a great cry. The sentinel watching the courtyard will rush to the opposite wall, to see me piled up on the terrace, with a length of rope in my hand. I shall plainly have fallen down while attempting to scale the wall. Mr. Chandos will be kneeling beside me, trying to lift me up. The sentry will rush to his tower to raise the alarm. He will surely leave the door open—the door from the roof. *Mr. Hanbury and Bell and Rowley will immediately cross the roof and follow him in.*

"Now I think that Rose Noble will go to the terrace at once; and the others with him. You see, if I were to die, Mrs. Pleydell, comparatively speaking, would hardly pay for her keep. So I think they'll all get down to me as fast as they can. Very well. While they are gone, Mr. Hanbury, Rowley and Bell will find Mrs. Pleydell, release her and carry her off. Let her down to the spur with Rowley and see that she runs for the wood. Carson to drive her to Poganec there and then. *Not until she's down on the spur* will Mr. Hanbury and Bell return to the tower—with the object of killing Rose Noble before he kills them."

He paused there for a moment, biting his lip.

"I don't like it," he added slowly, "but I don't know what else to do. It washes me out of the battle and Mr. Chandos, too; but a part must be played which no one but we two can play. Rose Noble has got to be drawn from his prisoner's side. And nothing that I can think of will do that, except my health. Any ordinary demonstration would make him stick tighter than ever to Mrs. Pleydell's arm. But tell him I'm down and out, and, though he won't believe you, *he'll go to see.* And on that point, one word more.

"Instead of rushing to the terrace, Rose Noble might rush to the roof. He's a very shrewd man. If he does, you've got him, you three. Don't wait. Just let him have it—both barrels and one for luck. Once he's over, you won't see the others for dust."

As he spoke, some door was opened, and down the

winding stairway came Punter's voice.

"An', when you're through, you might take a look at the Willie. I don't suppose he'd bite you if you took out his bit."

"Rose said—" began Casemate.

"I know," said Punter. "That's Rose. But I don't fancy dead men. You can shove the corpse in the ground, but a yard full of sextons can't bury the ——— shout. One or two dead's enough, and before this worry's over you'll see all that. No. Let the ——— waste if you like, but keep 'im alive."

At Punter's first word we had begun to withdraw, for it had been arranged that, at the first show of movement, we should immediately enter the room which Adèle had used. At a sign from Mansel, however, I let the others retire and began to follow him gently up the stair. This was, of course, of stone, so we made no sound.

It was a desperate move, but I knew where Mansel was going and I knew he was right to go.

Casemate was bound for the kitchen; so Casemate had to be stopped. And, if he reached the guard-room before us, the game was up. You cannot pursue in silence over a wooden floor.

Mercifully the voices continued, but I never knew what they said. My ears were strained to catch nothing but a step on the stair.

But none came. Only the voices grew clearer the higher we went.

We glided into the guard-room, after the way of a snake. Then we turned right and left and stood, one on each side of the doorway, with our backs flat against the wall. The wicket opened outwards, so we were very well placed.

"I don't care," Casemate was saying, "I don't like

the ———— job. I don't mind dirty weather, but I like to know where I am."

"If you must know," said Punter, "you're up on the velvet top. Mansel put up a bluff, and its bottom's fell out. Rose has got 'im as tight as a—"

"Never knew when he hadn't," said Casemate. "First, he'd never find us; and then he'd never get in. Now you say 'That's all right, but he'll never get out.' An' what about Jute? Where's Jute?"

"Jute knows 'is garden," said Punter. "If Jute don't come in, it's because there's some rhubarb wants watchin' the other side."

"If you ask me," said Casemate, "Jute's ———— *well pulled out.*"

"Oh, put it away," said Punter. "Why, Jute—"

"———— well pulled out," repeated Casemate. "He's had a look at his seaweed and he's got in out of the rain. An' I don't blame 'im. 'Half a million,' says Rose, 'for the pickin' up.' *'Pickin' up.'*" He sucked in his breath. "I wonder what he'd call 'reachin' down.' An' when I said 'Who's this Mansel?,' he says, 'He's a one-legged Willie, with a college way of talking and a mouth full of rubber teeth.'"

"Now, look 'ere," said Punter earnestly. "I don't deny that Mansel's not big small stuff. He ran round Jute, an' he climbs like a ———— ape. But that's where 'e gets off. He's not up to Rose's weight."

"He never was," said Casemate. "But he ———— near got him down; an' he's not dead yet."

"Now look at it this way," said Punter, plainly doing his best to hearten his doubting friend. "A man don't cough up half a million because you tickle 'is chin. He's got to be broke in pieces, an' then some more. Well, he's not going to hand you the funny 'ammer, you know. He's goin' to bite an' scratch—till you've got him stuck. Well, he's had his bite an' his scratch, an' now he's ——— well stuck. I'll tell you this. So long as Mansel was out, I never slep' sound. I've seen 'im before, an' I like to know 'is game. But now I'll put my feet up, because the ———'s stuck, ——— well stuck, like a bug pinned up on a board. An' you watch 'im come unbuttoned this afternoon. Wait till he hears the goods beginning to talk."

"It doesn't hurt," said Casemate. "I had my arm done once."

"I guess Rose didn't do it," said Punter. "And now slip after them eats. There's a pot o' strawberry back o' the cans of pears."

Casemate made no answer, but began to descend....

I think I shall always hear his steps on the stair.

To my fancy his tread seemed wary, as thought the man were suspicious, apprehensive of ill to come. He certainly stood at the wicket for a quarter of a minute or more, as though he had remarked and was listening to the vigorous slam of my heart two paces away.

Then he pulled open the door and came into the room.

I did not see Mansel strike him, for the former had been a great boxer and was startlingly quick with his hands. But I heard the dull smack of the blow, and I saw Casemate spin on his heel and then fall away from me backwards, without a cry. I heard his head meet the stone, and his body fell down with a thud, but the sounds were dead sounds and could not, I think, have been heard at the head of the stair.

My eyes were still upon Casemate, when Mansel touched me and turned.

I pointed to the form on the floor.

"Safe for an hour," breathed Mansel. "The others will tie him up."

We whipped down into the gallery, and, whilst I summoned the others, Mansel undid the bolts of the passage door.

I must here confess that I quailed at the sight of that suite. For me it reeked of misfortune, of frantic endeavour doomed before it was begun; and to go back to such a cockpit of broken hopes was clean against my stomach. Yet, as Mansel had said, there was nothing else to be done; and, in view of the Casemate business, we had not a moment to lose.

I signed to Rowley to give me his coil of rope.

As he laid it about my shoulders,

"Shut the door, but don't bolt it," breathed Mansel. "And stand by to move in five—not ten minutes' time."

Hanbury nodded. I observed that he looked very pale.

Then Mansel stole into the passage, and I in his wake.

Before we had gained the Closet, the door had been shut.

The windows of the Closet were still open, as was the trap-door, and the room was full of sweet air and the murmur of the water below.

Mansel sat down on the floor and swung his legs into the trap. Then he looked up and smiled.

"William," he said, keeping his eyes upon mine, "we're going to bring this right off. I know you're frightened to death of letting me down; but you won't—if you do as I say.

"I want you to stand at that window, and I'll tell you what you will see. Never mind whether you're dreaming or whether your sight is blurred. *This is what you will see*—and, consequently, what you will do.

"You'll see me come out of the archway on to the

terrace below. You'll see me cast the rope and you'll watch it rise. At the second attempt you'll see it catch on something—you can't tell what. You'll see me test it and watch me begin to climb. I shall go up...up... up...Leaning well out of the window, you'll watch me with your heart in your mouth. When I'm six feet from the top, *to your indescribable horror* the rope will begin to slip. Instinctively you'll try to warn me—let out a hell of a cry. As you do so, the rope will go, and I shall come down. You'll see me asprawl on the terrace, lying appallingly still and you'll naturally rush to reach me as quick as you can. I shall be plainly disabled— for all you know, dead. Well, that means the game's over, and you'll naturally shout for help. When it comes, they may possibly seize you, but you'll only do your best to get back to my side. You see, I shall still be breathing, but the fall will have broken my back.

"And now let me have the rope.

"When you see my arm go back, you'll know that I'm going to sling it. Watch it rise and fall, and mark how I gather it up for the second cast."

As he spoke, he was making a slip-knot, but his eyes never left my face.

Then he smiled again and disappeared.

I made my way to the window, like a man in a dream...

I cannot swear to what happened in the next two minutes of time. That is the plain truth. Time and again I have called up the burden of those moments, started to set it down and then laid aside my pen. I remember it perfectly; but I cannot say "This I imagined, and that I saw," for the line between fact and fancy is a line that I cannot trace. Indeed I shall always believe that Mansel had influenced my will, for I did what I did dazedly and was conscious all the time of the smile upon Mansel's face and the light in his eyes.

I remember leaning out of the window and finding the air most heavy and the sunshine curiously dull; I remember how the sill of the casement punished my back and how the sweat was running upon my hands and face; I remember shrieking incoherence and feeling suddenly sick and staggering down to the archway trembling in every limb....

And then I was all dripping wet and down on my knees, and Mansel lay huddled before me with one leg beneath the other and a loose look about his neck.

I got my arm under his shoulders and raised him up, but his head rolled over sideways and, though I tried to prop it, it would not stay.

I cried out at that, but maybe I had shouted before, for I saw Rose Noble coming, with Punter and Bunch. They seemed to come down in a wave—down the steps from a door in the wall.

As they reached the terrace, a slim figure flashed in their wake. I watched it outstrip the three men...thrust them aside....

Then Adèle was down beside me and sitting back on her heels, with agony in her eyes and Mansel's hand in her lap.

8

Out of Sight, Out of Mind

The shutting of a door roused me, and I sat up to find myself alone.

The mountain-tops before me were alight with sunshine, and in the huge void which lay between them and the terrace a great bird was sailing and wheeling, as an aeroplane at play.

For a moment I watched it lazily. Then I remembered with a shock the plan we had laid and how perfectly it had worked and how, in the moment of triumph, Adèle had brought it to nought.

In a flash, I was on my feet, and trying to think what to do.

I had been left in a faint, not so much as bound. My pistol had been taken, but not my knife. It was clear that I was regarded as safe under lock and key.

At this my heart leaped up, for, of course, I could leave by the suite whenever I pleased: the only question was how to turn to account this unsuspected freedom.

In view of the turn events had taken, Mansel was sure to continue his pretence of a broken back; finding their purpose frustrated, George and the servants were probably lying concealed in the south-east tower; I was at liberty, and the enemy was clean off his guard. If we had shot at a pigeon, we had killed something more than a crow. We had made notable progress, and, before the day was over....

And there I remembered Casemate, and my dreams began to settle, as a house that is built upon sand.

Casemate's failure to return would ruin everything.

Quite apart from the finding of him senseless, which might any moment take place, the instant Rose Noble learned that Casemate was not up to time, his ever-smouldering suspicion would burst into flame. He would see in a twinkling that here was our handiwork, and, with Mansel under his hand, would turn the tables upon us before we could think.

With a hammering heart, I ran to the channel and fought my way under the door. If I could do nothing else, at least I could get hold of Casemate and carry him out of sight. And, in any event, I was plainly better at large than cooped, like a dog, on the terrace, at the mercy of any whim that came into the enemy's head.

A moment later I was standing in the "gallery of stone"....

Casemate lay as we had left him, flat on his back.

To my surprise, he was neither gagged nor bound; then I remembered that we had never told George to tie him up. And I had no cord....

I carried him out of the guard-room and along a passage by which we had come from the porch. There I found a bedroom that had not been used. I was preparing to thrust him under the bed and was wondering what fool had coined the saying "Out of sight, out of mind," and whether, had he known Rose Noble, the adage would not have been revised, when another proverb came thrusting into my mind.

A living dog, saith The Preacher, *is better than a dead lion.*

And that made me think of the fable of the ass in the lion's skin.

And out of the two came wisdom, if you can call it such.

Richard William Chandos, alive and in Casemate's clothes, would be infinitely better than Casemate as good as dead. *Casemate could not return; but Chandos in Casemate's clothes could be seen in the porch....*

And here another idea leaped into my mind.

Casemate had been uneasy—had said so in so many words. "I don't like the job." Punter had done his utmost to lay his fears, but the other would not be comforted, rebutting each effort of Punter's with some unpleasant truth. More, Casemate clearly believed that Jute had seen breakers ahead and had left the ship.

"And I don't blame him." Was it incredible, then, that Casemate should follow Jute's lead? Open the castle gate, which he had to pass, slip out and up to the wood and so wash his hands of a business which he very plainly wished he never had touched? Even if he were not seen going, *the open gate would account for his failure to reappear.*

In less than three minutes Casemate was under the bed, and I was clad in his suit. This was none too clean and something tight; but I liked it better than his hat, which fitted me very well.

Now, though in this time much had happened, it was barely a quarter of an hour since Casemate had parted from Punter at the head of the stair. I had, therefore, a very good hope of suggesting that Casemate had flitted before he was due to return; but our hopes had so often foundered that, for all my haste, I stole, like a thief, from the bedroom, and went with my chin on my shoulder until the passage gave way to a flight of stairs.

So I came to the porch.

The courtyard was empty, and so, to my relief, was the roof. For a moment I found this strange; then I remembered that, when I had come to my senses, the rope which had lain on the terrace was no longer there, and, since without rope I could not descend from a window, it was plainly needless to post a sentinel.

At once I whipped to the gate and drew the great bolts. Then I set aside the shutter which masked the grill and, after a glance behind me, pulled the great leaf open and stepped outside.

I can never remember that moment without emotion.

The sparkle of the wet, green turf and the brilliant foliage beyond, the gay singing of the birds and the sweet smell of the earth filled me with a sudden amazement, as though I had clean forgotten that such things were. Yet, only three days before, I had drunk my fill of them. Which shows, I think, that the burden of those three days was even more exacting than we had guessed.

When I looked back through the grill, there was still no one to be seen; so, quick as a flash, I slipped back into the porch and, leaving the great door ajar, entered the doorway which stood in the eastern wall.

I was a little uneasy about the gate, for, to serve my purpose, it should stay so much open as to attract the eye; but this was the very thing which Casemate, deserter, would have done his best to avoid. Still, he could have done no more than draw it to, and, even while I stood thinking, the fresh north-westerly breeze took the matter out of my hands. At its instance the massive leaf began very slowly to move and had very soon swung so far that none that looked into the courtyard could ever have missed its tale.

Now all this was well enough; when his fellows began to wonder where Casemate could be, an excellent answer was staring them in the face; but a sudden fear came upon me lest Casemate himself should suddenly come to his senses and, rising as it were from the dead, offer a still better answer to his inquisitive friends. Mansel had said that he would be "safe" for an hour; but it might very well be that more than an hour would elapse before we could afford to ignore the chance of his coming to life. And here, for the first time—fear, I suppose, breeding fear—I began to grow uneasy about the condition of things in the south-east tower.

I glanced at my watch.

Fifteen minutes had passed since I had sat up on the terrace to find myself alone. Yet there had been no action of any sort. I had seen no movement and I had heard no sound. We were four fit men to three, while the enemy thought they were three to one dying man.

The odds were full in our favour. Yet, though time was precious, no blow had been struck.

As I stood, biting my fingers, the answer came into my mind. There was but one explanation—the old familiar stile was still barring our way. *Neither Mansel nor George nor the servants had been able to come between Rose Noble and Adèle.* Close as they were to this bourne, the other's devilish instinct was holding them up; and, until this relaxed or the monster flew in its face, they dared not move.

Now that, I confess, was guesswork, but this was clear. Could they have done it, Mansel or George or both would have struck fifteen minutes ago. They had not, because they could not; and, if they could not then, God alone knew how long they would have to wait.

And that brought me back to Casemate. "Safe for an hour." Why, two, three, six hours might not be enough....

Now, though I could gag the man, I had no cord; and without cord I could not bind him as such a man should be bound. I, therefore, opened the door in the eastern wall of the archway in some hope of finding the storeroom to which Casemate had been dispatched.

The door led into a chamber which was clearly the porter's lodge.

On either side of the window, which was some way above the ground, were steps leading up two stalls, cut out of the wall, from which the porters could comfortably watch the spur. Facing the window was a door, with a key in its lock. I guessed at once that this led to the caretaker's room, or, at least, to the room in which they were now confined, for I had no doubt that they had been shut in their quarters, and these were sure to be within sound of the gate. A third door stood open, revealing a passage and staircase, both of stone....

Five rooms I entered, but, though I rummaged desperately, I could not light on so much as a foot of cord, or, for the matter of that, of any substitute. Not daring to wait any longer, I decided to make my way back, and, ripping the tick from a mattress, to tear this into strips and bind Casemate with those.

I, therefore, hastened back to the porch, but, before I crossed to the doorway in the opposite wall, I naturally put out my head to see that the coast was clear.

The roof was empty, but, standing in the courtyard, some ten or twelve paces away, was an elderly man. His back was towards me, but the cut of his clothes was not English, and, when he moved his head, I could see the shanks of spectacles resting above his ears. He was plainly hot, for he had his hat in his hand and was mopping his face, but he looked about him placidly and with evident relish, as a man who has made an effort and is content with his reward.

Then he turned suddenly about, and I knew him at once.

It was the bookseller of Lass.

To tell the truth, I was not greatly surprised.

The guide the old fellow had written showed very plainly his veneration for Gath; when he kept holiday, therefore, that he should visit the spur was natural enough; and though to walk seven miles to look at a castle wall may be the way of a zealot, I imagine his tastes were simple and his pleasures were few.

And so he had come to the spur to look upon Gath.

Finding the gate open, he had naturally seized the chance to make his way in and once more enjoy a prospect from which he had been lately debarred.

But, if I was not surprised, I was considerably moved.

Such was the emplacement of the castle, so thick was the wood that masked the spur and so lonely was the country round about that we had all come to ignore the chance of an outsider's entry upon the scene. This was now, however, an accomplished fact. A respectable citizen of Lass, an intelligent man, well acquainted with Gath and with its ownership, was actually within the walls and must already have found the open gate and the absence of any custodian matters for serious remark. More. His eyes had only to light upon George Hanbury, Bell or myself, when his suspicions would be instantly quickened by that most lively curiosity which our use of his apartment at Lass and our strange and precipitate departure must have aroused.

And here it seemed that Fortune was at last inclining towards our part, for, while the bookseller's presence could do us no harm, the last thing Rose Noble desired was a witness of what was afoot.

Now all this swept through my mind in a tenth of the time it has taken to set it down, but right on the heels of this valueless speculation came a fair, clean-cut idea, upon which, for once, I had the good sense to act without any hesitation or weighing of odds.

The bookseller had not seen me, but I stepped out into his view. He looked very much surprised, but, before he could speak, I beckoned him to follow and, crossing to the opposite doorway, led the way to a corner below some stairs.

"Look at me well," I whispered. "Have you ever seen my before?"

He replied directly that I was one of the strangers that had made some use of the parlour above his shop.

"That's right," said I. "And now, before I tell you how and why I come to be here, answer me this. Would you like to help a lady who goes in danger of death?"

"I would indeed," said the bookseller stoutly enough.

"Then listen," said I.

As shortly as ever I could, I told him a few of the facts. He heard me solemnly, with his big, blue eyes on my face.

"So you see," I said, in the end, "it's a business of life and death. You're not safe here. No one is; but a stranger, least of all. I'd be very glad of your help, but I'm bound to tell you that the only help you can give will involve you in a terrible risk."

"Thank you," said the bookseller politely. "Please tell me what I may do."

His calm firmness of purpose took me by storm; of pure gratitude I could have gone on my knees.

"In the first place," said I, "you're a doctor—remember that. A doctor out for the day. Hanbury met you in the road at the end of the drive. You can describe him, can't you? The man who bought *Alison's Europe* and borrowed your coat and hat. Very well. He asked you if you knew of a doctor, and when he heard you were one he begged you to come here at once. He said that you'd find the gate open and told you how to get to the south-east tower. There, he said, was a man very grievously hurt.

"Now that is the tale you will tell, when you get to the room; but, before you get so far, I think the fat man you find there will have rushed upstairs to the roof. The 'open gate' will fetch him, if nothing else. If he stays where he is, please pretend to examine the man who is lying hurt; take off his coat and shirt and feel his spine; then announce that his back is broken, but that, if he lies flat and still, he may possibly live. Then ask the fat man if he will kindly see if your son has arrived; say that *he was to follow you here as soon as he'd changed his tire.* That'll move the fat man all right. You see we've got to get him out of the tower."

"Sir," said the bookseller gravely, "it shall be done."

"It's a dangerous game," said I. "If he thinks that you're lying, the fat man will shoot you dead."

The old fellow smiled.

"I am old," he said simply. "And lonely. Since my wife was dead, I do not much value my life. But you and your lady are young. . . . And, besides, I do not think he will think I am lying—this fat man of yours."

"He's pretty shrewd," said I.

"Let us go, please," said the bookseller, settling his hat on his head. . . .

We had almost reached the guard-room and I had stopped to listen for any sound, when I heard the scamper of feet upon the roof.

The murder was out, and Punter or Bunch was running to shut the gate.

Mercifully the door of the bedroom in which I had hidden Casemate was less than ten paces away, so I opened it quickly and thrust the bookseller in. As I closed it behind me, I heard a flurry of footsteps and the clack of the guard-room wicket flung back against the wall.

Now, as I have said, the guard-room's floor was of stone; but the floor of the passage which followed was of oak boards that had been polished and highly waxed; and, since whoever was coming was running as fast as he could, I was not surprised that so soon as he left the guard-room and trod the oak, he slipped and lost his footing and took the deuce of a fall.

For a moment there was dead silence. Then I heard Punter's voice.

If he omitted any blasphemies, I cannot think what they were; he stayed quite still, vomiting a stream of imprecation and only interrupting his recital to groan with pain.

In the midst I heard other steps coming, and almost at once Bunch spoke.

"What's up?" said he. "Took a toss?"

"Oh, no," said Punter shakily. "Just 'avin' a lil lay down. 'Toss,' you gentle——? I wish I'd got the —— that shined these boards."

"It's comin' after the stones," said Bunch sententiously. "That's wot it is. You nips off of the stones on to—"

"My God," screeched Punter, "don't I know what you does? Ain't I jus' done it, you ——?"

"All right, all right," said Bunch soothingly. "But you ain't broke nothing, an' wot about shuttin' the gate?"

"—— the gate," said Punter. "An' Casemate—the dirty swine. I knew the —— was windy, but I never dreamed he was down to doin' a bunk."

"That's Jute," said Bunch. "'E would 'ave it Jute 'ad beat, an' 'e thought the devil o' Jute."

"God knows why," said Punter bitterly. "It's Jute tore everything up. If 'e 'adn't let Mansel bounce 'im, we'd 've been in Paris by now—'avin' our breakfast in bed, with our cheque books under our arms. 'Alf a million o' money, an' nothin' said. An' now you can 'ave my bit for a double Scotch."

"'E ain't dead yet," said Bunch.

"He's broke his back," said Punter. "Rose knows it better than us."

"Then, why's 'e waitin'?" said Bunch. "Sittin' there like a—policeman by the side o' the bed?"

"You can search me," said Punter. "I don't think 'e knows 'imself. But it's no good sayin' nothin'—es just black ice. I thought the goods was dead when she slipped 'er cuff."

There was a gloomy silence.

Then—

"Come on," said Bunch. "Best shut that —— gate."

The other got to his feet, and the two passed on.

I could hardly believe my ears when I heard the two

of them making towards the porch. Here was a stroke of luck for which I had never hoped. And then I saw with shock how wretched a plotter I was, for, with Punter and Bunch to waylay him, the "doctor" would never have won to the room in which Mansel lay.

The bookseller was speaking.

"I have understood nothing," he said; "only Rose is your lady's name."

"All slang," said I. "Thieves talk. Never mind," and, with that, I opened the door.

Swiftly we passed through the guard-room and climbed the winding stair which led to the roof.

This was empty, and, now that I could see all around, seemed like the pleasance of some god-philosopher, whence he could watch and contemplate the world. The place did not seem like a roof, but like a gigantic terrace, hung in the air. Even the chimney-stacks could not disturb this illusion, for they had no chimney-pots and might have been great pedestals ready for statuary which had not yet been done. Indeed, the extraordinary prospect troubled my head, and I felt suddenly dizzy and the palms of my hands grew wet.

The sun was high now, and the shadow of the south-east tower lay sharp upon the flags. The stacks, too, threw their shadows and the battlements made a pattern along the side.

As I was peering, I heard the hollow clap of the castle gate....

A moment later we were standing by the door of the south-east tower.

"I'm afraid I can't tell you," I breathed, "which room they'll be in; but I think you'll find it leads out of the 'gallery of stone.'"

The bookseller nodded, and I put out my hand.

This seemed to please him, for he took it in both of his. Then he put his mouth to my ear.

"I go," he whispered, "to betray the violator of Gath."

Then he adjusted his spectacles, nodded, smiled and disappeared.

Now, if I had had a pistol, I should have stayed by the door, to kill Rose Noble as he stepped on to the roof. But my pistol had been taken, and Casemate had carried no arms. I certainly had my knife, but I dared not trust my handling of such a weapon to make an end of such a man. I have often thought since that here I made a mistake and that I should have stabbed the monster as he came out of the door, but up to that day I had never done any worse violence than knock a man down with my fist, and I was frankly afraid of making a mess of the business and thereby wrecking the ship which I was trying to steer.

I, therefore, whipped to the nearest chimney-stack and crouched, with this between me and the southeast tower. This stack was to be my shield. As Rose Noble came by, I would move, keeping it always directly between him and me, and, when he was by, I would dash for the south-east tower. Once within, I had but to shut the door and shoot the bolts to bring us over the bar which had balked us so long. The rest would be child's play. If five men armed could not break out at their pleasure.... It occurred to me suddenly that, if there was no way by the chapel, Mansel would bring out Adèle through the Dining-room floor.

Looking back, I find it curious that I should have had no doubt that Rose Noble would come up to the roof. That nine men out of ten would have done so is nothing at all. Rose Noble was the tenth man in all that he did. I cannot pay him a higher compliment. Yet I never had any doubt that, once my decoy was in action, our enemy would fall into the pit which I had digged. I was certain of this as if I had seen it written among the orders of Fate. This by the grace of God, for upon that certainty was founded the whole of my simple plan and, had I stopped to consider how bold was my postulate, I am sure that my judgment would have faltered and that I should have abandoned my design as out of reason.

Rose Noble came up quietly, without any haste. Had I not been expecting to hear them, I should not have heard his steps. I had thought that he would come running crying for Punter or Bunch. But he did not. Rather he seemed to be prowling, like some suspicious beast.

For a moment he paused on the opposite side of my stack, for all the world as though he had heard me move. Then he went on his way to the south-west tower.

I let him take ten paces. Then I rounded the stack and made my dash for the door.

And here, I think, my heart stood suddenly still.

The door was shut; and when I lifted the latch, I found it was barred.

For an instant I stared at it blankly. Then the truth rose up in a blinding flash.

Knowing nothing of me, Mansel had followed Rose Noble up the stair and had played my hand before I could play it myself.

The game was won—over: Adèle was saved; Rose Noble had been "caught bending"; *and so had I.*

A slight noise made me look round.

Rose Noble was standing, glaring, six paces away.

His face was working and his hand in his jacket-pocket was twitching with wrath. I think that he would have spoken, for twice he opened his mouth; but his fury must have choked him, for, though he gaped upon me, the words seemed stuck in his throat.

He was never a pleasant sight, but, so transfigured,

he made as dreadful a picture as ever I saw, and I must confess that, as I looked upon him, my blood ran cold.

I was sure he was going to kill me, if only to serve his rage, for he knew as well as did I who it was that had shut the door and that Mansel, while he lay at his mercy, had bluffed him into discarding a winning hand. Indeed, had he guessed that George and the servants were actually in the tower, he would I believe, have shot me down like a dog; but, as the moments went by, yet he did not fire, I began to believe that he had still some hope of saving the game, and, since I was plainly his prisoner, had decided to hold me alive to his future use.

In a word, I was pretty desperate; but the thought of the part I had played in bringing him down did my heart good, and, what is more, it served to steady my nerves and to set my brain working to see if I could not hold out until help should come.

I folded my arms, leaned against the wall of the tower and waited for Rose Noble to speak.

At length—

"How did you get here?" he said.

"Thanks to Hanbury," said I. "He opened the passage door."

In a flash he had me by the collar and a pistol was hurting my ribs.

"March," he said thickly.

Together we crossed the roof and entered the opposite tower. Then we went down the stair to the "gallery of stone." He held me to the wall with the pistol, while he bolted the passage door. An instant later we were back on the roof.

"How did you come by those clothes?"

"Mine were wet," said I. "And, as Casemate didn't need them—"

"Why didn't he need them?"

"Because Hanbury had laid him out."

The man's eyes burned in his head. They seemed to be striving to bore their way into my brain. Though he suspected it deeply, he could find no fault in my tale.

After a little he stepped to the balustrade.

"Bunch! Punter!" he roared.

For a moment he stood still, waiting, then he leaned over the stone.

"Come here," he cried.

Again he waited, like a great beast about to spring.

"Look in that ——— kitchen and see if it's all O.K."

There was a moment's silence; then I heard a scared voice.

"'E's gone!" cried Punter.

Rose Noble drew himself up and turned to me.

"Where's Hanbury now?"

"I don't know," said I. "He went to get the servants, but he hasn't come back."

"Why not?" said Rose Noble.

"I don't know," said I. "I was waiting to let them in, when the doctor appeared. So I left the gate open and came straight up to the roof."

"I shouldn't lie," said Rose Noble.

Before I could answer, Punter appeared on the roof.

"Rose," he said, "Casemate's—"

There he saw me and stopped dead, with his mouth and his eyes wide open and a hand half way to his head.

Grimly Rose Noble surveyed him.

"Well, what of Casemate?" he said.

Dazedly Punter regarded him. Then he pointed to me.

"'E's done 'im in," he said stupidly. "Look at 'is ——— soot."

170

The wretched man was plainly thinking aloud, but Rose Noble was not in the mood to receive such gifts. He did not actually strike him, but he took him by the shoulders and shook him, till he wore the colour of death and I really thought that his brains must be loose in his head. Then he flung him away against the wall of the tower, and using a frightful oath, demanded the truth.

At first Punter could not speak. Then he put a hand to his temples and moistened his lips.

"I thought he'd beat it," he faltered. "When I saw the ——— gate open—"

"When was this?"

"Why, jus' now," said Punter. "I'd only that moment shut it, when you called me down."

Rose Noble was plainly uncertain what to think.

My tale was unlikely enough, but the facts bore it out. That I should have quitted the porch before George and the servants were safely within the castle seemed to him a mistake which not even a child would have made. Yet, if they were truly within, a child would have had the good sense to shut the gate. Of these two incredible conclusions he did not know which to choose, and, as I watched his teeth at work on his lower lip, I was elated to think that I had contrived to embarrass so subtle a brain.

My triumph was short-lived.

"I guess Hanbury's only two hands—and those were fast. How did you make the kitchen out of that flat?"

The thrust was so unexpected that I could only stare.

"Speak up, you young fool," said Rose Noble. "I saw the way he was tied."

I swallowed desperately. Lest Mansel should mean to use it, I dared not reveal the fact that the table sank through the floor.

"Out of the window," I said, "when the servants attacked. I went into the kitchen for shelter and found him there."

"Why didn't Mansel go with you?"

"He hadn't time," said I. "The light was back on the windows before he could follow me down."

"You knew the servants were there. Why didn't you go to the porch and let them in?"

"I tried to," said I. "But I didn't dare show a light and I couldn't undo the bolts."

"But you did in the end," said Rose Noble, rubbing his nose. "That's why that attack was a washout. You whistled 'em down from the roof and handed them in. Are you sure you got out by the window?"

A sudden belief that the man was playing with me sent the blood to my head. In a trice I had lost my temper and found my tongue.

"Have it your own way," said I. "It won't be for long. I may have played the hand badly, but I've made the odd trick. You're the wrong side of the door, and we can afford to wait. That doctor comes out of Lass, and, if he's not back by sundown, I fancy his friends and relations will wonder why."

Now, if this was all Greek to Punter, it was so much gall to his chief. Servants within or without, so long as Mansel sat still, he could not act, and, unless he acted quickly, the chance would pass. The stranger within the gates had set the sand-glass up, and the grains which had lain so long idle had now begun to run. And nothing on earth could stop them. Happen what might, before many hours were over tongues would be wagging and eyes would be turning to Gath. Before any steps were taken, if Rose Noble valued his freedom, he would be wise to be gone.

But, if I had stung him, the monster gave no sign.

"Yes," he said slowly, "I guess I shall have it my way."

The words were softly spoken, but his tone was so dark and so sinister that I found them more disturbing than any explosion of wrath. Indeed, his whole demeanour seemed to have changed: the red heat of passion was gone, and, in its stead, a coldness which was not human possessed this terrible man. And, if that did not show me, the next ten minutes declared why men endured his service and went in fear of his name.

He never once used an oath or two words where one would serve, and, if a sign could take the place of an order, he made a sign. He never hesitated or gave any sort of reason for the commands he gave; himself he did nothing and seemed t˜ be oblivious of what was done, yet, when Bunch was about to gag me, he had knocked me down before I knew myself that my hand had instinctively moved towards my knife. No Pharoah could have been more imperious, no beast so vigilant, nothing but a statue could have stood so still and cold. What was far more, the man compelled belief. That I had duped him was forgotten; if he said "Shut that door," I knew that to leave it open would have been a fatal mistake; he gave the impression of providing for what was coming to pass; from his orders alone you could foretell the future, till looking ahead seemed as simple as looking back. Little wonder that Bunch and Punter hung on his lips....

Casemate was found and heartily soused with water in a hope of bringing him to, but Mansel had struck too well, and after a little they left him to fare as best he could. I was gagged and my wrists were tightly bound. Food and wine were packed in a battered bag and, without passing through the porch, we left by a lower window and gained the spur.

This was of course, the window by which Hanbury had been brought in. The middle bar could be lifted, so that a man could pass. The contrivance was simple, but none from without could have reached the plate, like a damper, which locked the bar into place.

With never a look behind him, Rose Noble passed up the spur and into the drive. Once out of sight of the castle, he turned to the right and, plunging into the thicket, swung back towards the castle, till he came to a little hollow, sunk in the midst of bushes and overspread with the branches of the surrounding trees.

We were now on the fringe of the wood, and I could see the castle between the leaves; the drive was ten paces away and the spur but three, but, while we commanded both, a man must have stumbled upon us before he knew we were there.

Rose Noble pushed back his hat and lit a cigar.

Then—

"Watch," he said shortly and flung himself down on the turf.

Without a word, Bunch wriggled into the foliage, until he could see the spur, while Punter opened the bag and began to eat. Of me they took no notice, and, since it seemed idle to stand, I sat myself down. This miserably enough, for my bodily state was wretched and my heart was heavy as lead. If ever a man "meant business," Rose Noble was he, and there was death in the hollow for whoever came up to the drive. Carson was doomed; the cars were as good as gone; and I was the wretched decoy to draw Mansel out of the castle and into the snare. I could see it all coming as clearly as though it were past and could do no more to prevent it than one of those careless butterflies that we had passed on the spur.

Presently I laid down my head and stared at the sky.

At least the place was lovely, and the day as fine and smooth as a day could be. The fluting of birds and the steady hum of insects soothed the ear; and the wet grass was cool and fragrant against my cheek.

My head was aching, and I was parched with thirst; the gag was most hard on my jaws and my wrists were already sore; but I was very tired, and, since Nature is a governess not easily put about, the murmur of insects grew more and more slumberous, and, after a little space, I fell asleep.

"I reckon he's sweating," said Rose Noble.

I was wide awake in an instant. With the tail of my eye I could see that, except that Bunch was eating and Punter had taken his place, nothing had changed.

"Sweating blood," said Rose Noble. "One Willie up on the drop, and, unless he gets a move on, the other walks into our arms as soon as it's dark."

"Complete with car," said Bunch, licking his lips.

Rose Noble shrugged his shoulders.

"Maybe," he said. "But I guess they'll give us the cars before we're through."

Punter looked down from his post on the lip of the dell.

"He can lay to meeting 'is Gawd, if he comes out."

"That's why he's sweating," said Rose Noble. "This ——— garden's all right from the castle wall, but it's just a shade too wild for a good close-up."

"Suicide 'All," said Bunch. "But 'e won't 'ave a dart by daylight. 'E knows—"

"Yes, he will," said Rose Noble. "He'll never wait ten hours, while his Willies are getting wet. He'll bring two o' the servants with him, an' they'll come right up in a line."

Punter looked round.

"Didn't we ought to spread, Rose?"

The other shook his head.

"Stop one, an' you stop the lot. Say we lay out a servant—well, what'll Big Willie do? Fall on his —— stomach an' pray to God. He's only the wood to shoot at, an' he's three down instead of two. An' that's when we move. By the time he's got his soul straight, I guess I'll be ready to flip a fly off his nose."

"You don' wan' to kill 'im," said Bunch. "If you—"

"'Kill him?'" breathed Rose Noble. "'Kill him?'" I could hear him suck in his breath. "No, I'm not going to kill him. And if I were you, I wouldn't so much as loose off, if you see his face—*in case you killed him,* for, if you did, by ——, I'd feed your tripe to a mongrel before your eyes."

A prudent silence succeeded this horrid threat, which was not so much spoken as snarled and suggested a return of the temper with which the monster was ridden a while before. For my part, I would have welcomed that cold, black mood, for now his manner argued a confidence so rich and ripe and lazy as made me twice as hopeless as I had been before.

"I'm going to sell him," said Rose Noble. "Hang him up on a wall of that court—expose him for sale ... with a bucket on either foot—the way they made 'Poky' remember the name of his 'bank.' If he won't buy himself in, I guess the Willies'll think when they see the weights. An' before we reach the reserve, I guess the goods will ask him to change his mind."

"But see here, Rose," said Punter. "They won't 'ave the cash to pay with, an' 'ow can we wait? That blasted chemist—"

"Who wants to wait?" said Rose Noble. "I'll take their —— word. Oh, I guess they've got false bottoms, the same as anyone else. I wouldn't trust Mansel a foot—if none of his like could hear. But let one of 'em pass his word in *front of his* —— *kind,* an' he hasn't the spunk to break it for fear they'll think he's a swab. That's what they mean when they talk of *Noblesse Oblige;* if you want plain English, *Don't let 'em see your dirt."*

The venom with which he uttered this ugly argument declared the deadly hatred he bore us all, and I could not help wondering what was the fellow's history, for he had a commanding presence and was by no means common, as Punter and Bunch, while his speech was constantly betraying a considerable education which for some unaccountable reason he seemed to despise.

Punter took a deep breath.

"This time to-morrow," he said, "we'll be on the —— road."

"Out of the country, you mean, and pushing for France."

Bunch looked up from his victuals.

"Wot price the Customs?" he said. "I'll shift the —— Rolls, but there's photos stuck on to 'er papers, an' I don' wan' to be asked why I'm drivin' a stolen car."

Rose Noble yawned.

"I guess we'll give one of the Willies a lift to France. They'll have to go back to London to raise the wind. An' he'll put us through the Customs—if we remember to ask him while Mansel's up on the wall."

Punter spoke over his shoulder.

"What 'Poky' was that you mentioned? There was a 'Poky' Barrett I saw in a Boston bar. But he was a little old screw, with a jerky leg."

Rose Noble laughed.

"'Poky' Barrett" he said, "is forty-two."

"Go on," said Punter incredulously.

"Forty-two," said Rose Noble. "But he had...an illness...not quite seven years ago..."

Somehow I got to my knees and tried to speak.

The three watched me curiously.

I threw myself down and rubbed my head on the ground in a wild endeavour to tear the gag from my mouth. I heard Punter laugh and say something about a dog. The attempt exhausted me and was utterly vain. When I got again to my knees, my face was streaming with sweat.

Rose Noble looked at me and lifted his lids.

"An illness," he said softly. "Some people might say 'an attack.' It changed him...unbelievably....And the jerky leg came on about the same time. You see, when he wouldn't answer, *somebody happened to touch his sciatic nerve.*"

With a bursting head, I flung myself back on the turf....

I can never describe the agony of that hour.

I knew that Mansel would come, and I knew he would come before dark. He would never wait for ten hours before starting to my relief; and Carson had to be saved from walking clean into a trap. He had not rope enough to go by the cliff—the spur was his only way. And so he would come...by daylight...up to the wood...If he came, he was doomed. He could be seen approaching for two hundred yards or more, and no cunning would ever avail him against an ambuscade. There was no scope for cunning. The wood was dense, while, except for four or five trees, the spur was bare. I had no hope for him, and, if I had, Rose Noble's air would have killed it, for he, the soul of prudence, was awaiting his enemy's coming with his hands, so to speak, in his pockets and his sword in the rack.

Of what was to follow his wounding, I tried not to think.

Whoever was with him would be taken alive or dead; and Carson would walk into the shambles soon after the sun had set. With me for spokesman, those that were left in the castle would be apprised of the truth, and no doubt, at dawn the next day Adèle and Hanbury and I would be pleading with prayers and fortunes for the life of a broken man. And so the play would finish— in a welter of blood and tears. Redress was not to be thought of: the chances of vengeance would not be worth taking up. Then The Law would step in, pick over the ghastly business, madden us all with its ritual, ask unanswerable questions and believe what it chose. A hideous publicity would follow: the names of Adèle and Mansel would be in everyone's mouth; reporters would cluster round Poganec; char-à-bancs would be run to The Castle of Gath....

In this affliction of spirit I again and again forgot my bodily distress. This was as well, for the gag choked me and had broken the sides of my mouth, my wrists seemed to be on fire, the pain in my head was raging, and I might have been covered with blankets, so fast was I streaming with sweat. At times I made sure I was sickening for some disease, but I think that it was the tightness as well of my clothing as my bonds which joined with the heat of the day, not only made me so hot, but caused my blood to rebel against such usage.

Bunch drained his bottle of wine and lay down to sleep. Before he did so, he took a scarf from his pocket and bound my feet, and so put out the spark of hope I had cherished that, when the moment came, I could hurl myself into the bushes and betray his danger to Mansel by means of the noise I made.

Rose Noble was speaking.

"I guess you'll remember to-day. It'll spoil the green-wood for you for the rest of your life. When you see the sun on the leaves and you hear the birds piping

179

around, I guess you'll remember to-day, and, when you remember, I reckon you'll wish it was raining and that the boughs were bare.

"May be it'll learn you something that they don't teach at Oxford or the school for pretty, young boys. *Stick to your ——— last. Live an' let live.* If somebody pulls your nose, go to the police. Keep your ——— tadpoles, an' watch 'em turn into frogs, but leave the deep-sea fishing to them that know....

"When Mansel climbed into that strongbox, he cut his throat. *He gave me this wood for the taking*—just the kind of damn-fool error a squirt like Mansel would make. The poor trash couldn't see that, if ever it got to a dog-fight, *the ——— that had this thicket was bound to win.*"

If the fellow's words enraged me, I think that they angered him.

He knew as well as did I that we could not have taken the castle and held the wood as well and that Mansel had had to stake all upon freeing Adèle; he knew that Mansel had taken trick after trick, though the game was not of his choosing and every card was marked—*that Mansel could still win the odd...and the game and the rubber and all...if he would but sit still in the castle and let Carson and me take our chance.* He had sought to belittle the man who in fourteen days had achieved what Rose Noble himself had believed three impossible feats, first of all finding a needle out of a bottle of hay, then seizing a very bastille and, finally, plucking his lady out of the lion's mouth. He had sought to diminish Mansel, and he had failed, because the facts were against him and he had no sort of material with which to build his case. This poverty made him wroth, and, could he have called back his words, I think he would. But since he could not, he started to curse and swear, reviling Mansel in filthy and blasphemous terms and working himself into a very passion, because, I fancy, he knew that with every execration he was, so to speak, but further exposing his sores.

Throughout this exhibition, Bunch was pretending slumber, and Punter never moved, whilst I, of course, lay as I was, for, now that my feet were bound, I could not stir.

At last the storm blew itself out, and, after a decent silence, Rose Noble turned to the future and left the past.

"I guess Jute'll bite his thumbs, when he finds we're gone."

Bunch propped himself on an elbow and let out an oath.

"Serve 'im ——— well right," he spouted, "the dirty goat. Sits down in that crooked village an' leaves us to get the wet. I know 'is ——— idea of keepin' the background warm. Oysters an' girls an' movies an' a skinful every night."

"He had his orders," said Rose Noble, "an' he's broken 'em twice. If he'd done as I told him, we shouldn't have had this fuss. But maybe it's as well. It don't amuse me to suckle an insubordinate ——— that's let me down."

This definite intimation that no claim by Jute would be paid was greeted by Punter and Bunch with the highest glee, partly, no doubt, because each was expecting to profit by such a rule, but mainly, I think, because they detested Jute and the thought of his losing his share did their hearts good. Indeed, had they known the truth—that Jute was no longer alive to lodge his claim, they could not have been better pleased. They crowded and giggled like children, abused the dead man with a relish which must have made him turn in his grave, and showed an impatience for action which all their approaching welfare had failed to inspire.

Punter shook his fist at the castle and cried aloud.

"Come out, you one-legged ———, and take your gruel."

"Easy now," said Rose Noble. "He knows that he's for the high jump, and I guess you'd straighten your tie before buying that hop."

"Rose," says Bunch, all of a twitter, "are you sure we'd better not spread? You know. Just in case—"

Rose Noble sat up.

"If and when I say so, but not before. What the hell's the use of spreading before they show up? Or even then?"

"None whatever," said Mansel.

Then a shot was fired just behind me, and Rose Noble fell back, staring, with the blood running into his eyes.

Himself, Mansel unbound me and took the gag from my mouth, while Carson and Bell, who were with him, stood covering Punter and Bunch—in a way, a needless precaution, for the two seemed stupefied and gazed about them slowly, as though they had just been translated into another world. And so, I suppose, in a sense, they had been, for Rose Noble was stone dead, shot through the brain.

When he saw the state of my mouth, Mansel drew in his breath. Then his hands went under my arms, and he lifted me up.

There was a rill in the wood—we had heard the fuss of its water, whenever we used the drive. This we sought in silence, for I was past speaking, and Mansel held his tongue. Indeed, he had his hands full, for though I could walk, I had lost my sense of balance and but for his arms, must have fallen a score of times.

The water revived me, but, when I would have spoken, Mansel stopped me at once.

"All in good time," said he. "Those swine must be disposed of, and the cord's way back with the cars. You will stay here and rest, and I'll come back and find you as soon as ever I can."

With that, he was gone, and I turned again to the water and drank my fill....

After a little, I lay back and gazed at the sky.

To tell the truth, I was thankful to be alone.

I had been just as much shaken as Punter and Bunch, and the world seemed out of focus to my labouring brain.

One moment the enemy was rampant, and the next Rose Noble was dead; before he had left the castle, Mansel had appeared in the wood; the inevitable had not happened, the impossible come to pass.

More than once an absurd fear seized me that it was all a dream, and, indeed, I was still uneasy when I heard a comfortable sound—the sigh of one of the Rolls.

Ten minutes later Tester was licking my face....

"It's very simple," said Mansel, filling a pipe. "The whole of the credit is yours. You cut the Gordian knot; and when, because of my failure, our case was ten times worse than it had been before, you pulled the whole show round and did the trick."

To this I demurred, but he brushed my protests aside.

"Listen," he said. "They carried me in and laid me down on a bed in the middle room of the tower. They took my pistol and knife, locked them up in a cupboard and took the key. *Then they locked every door, except the door to the roof and that of the room in which I lay*. Well, that washed out George and the servants, for they were in the oratory, very properly biding their time. Then they hand-cuffed Adèle to my bed-post, and, when she slipped out of the cuff, they clipped her ankle instead. Then Rose Noble sat down and watched me—from a chair at the foot of the bed. Adèle told me afterwards that he never took his hand from his pocket or his eyes from my face.... If you can conceive a tighter place than that, I'd like to hear what it is.

"Well, the 'doctor' appeared, and, before he'd said thirty words, Rose Noble was out of the room. When I rose to follow, Adèle almost bent it again. She started up, forgetting her ankle was fast to the leg of the bed. I just managed to catch her in time....

"I shut the door to the roof and started to look for the keys. I found them at last, high up in a niche in the wall. Then I unlocked the doors. I had no idea where George and the servants were, and, as luck would have it, I tried the oratory last. Not until then did I go back to the 'doctor' and ask about you. To my horror, I learned he had left you up on the roof....

"Of course I realized I had shut the door in your face, and, when I rushed back to listen, I could hear Rose Noble speaking and you reply. I took Bell's pistol, posted George and Rowley as best I could and cautiously opened the door, *to find that the roof was empty and the opposite door was shut*. This made me think very hard. Although he knew we had rope, Rose Noble was giving us the roof; but the gifts of a man like that are always dangerous, and I instantly wondered if he meant to take to the wood.

"A moment's reflection convinced me that this was so.

"In the first place, to use his own words, 'if ever it got to a dog-fight, the fellow that had this thicket was bound to win'; in the second, the dog-fight was coming—there was any amount to suggest that the servants were in; the castle would soon be unhealthy, because of the doctor's friends; and, then, the cars for the taking and Carson as well; finally, he knew I should seek you, and the very best place in which to hold you prisoner was, therefore, the wood.

"There was not a moment to lose. We couldn't go down the cliff, for we hadn't sufficient rope, and our only chance was to reach the wood by the spur not only before Rose Noble, *but before he was in a position to see us go.*

"I left George and Rowley with Adèle, who was now as safe as a house, and Bell and I slid down from the roof to the spur. The 'doctor,' a gallant old fellow, drew up the rope behind us and then slipped back to the tower. Believe me, I ran for this wood, with my heart in my mouth....

"When we made the drive, I sent Bell off for Carson and lay in wait. Almost at once you appeared. I watched you come out of the window and start for the wood, but, when I felt for my pistol, *it wasn't there....*

"I'd given it back to Bell, before I went down the rope, and in the rush I'd forgotten to ask for it back.

"Well, there was nothing to be done. I retired, marked you to cover and then went off to pick up Carson and Bell. I'm afraid the delay cost you dear, for I had to be careful to meet them a long way back and, of course, we had to come up without snapping a twig. But I think, perhaps, after all, it was better so, for the sprint had unsteadied my hand, and, if I had missed or anything else had slipped, you were a pretty good hostage and I was but one to three.

"The rest you know." He rose to his feet and stretched luxuriously. "And now, if you feel like moving, we'll get into one of the cars and go back to Adèle. Carson and Bell are digging a certain grave, I think we'll leave them to it—and him to them. To tell you the truth, I don't want to see him again. The sight of him rouses feelings that one shouldn't have against the dead. In his way, he was a great man, and, if he'd had the help I've had, he'd have wiped me off the map. He hadn't a servant worth having—they let him down right and left; he practically stood alone; and, even so, it took six of us all we knew to bring him down."

It is not for me to review that valediction; I heard it in silence, and in silence I leave it now. The quarrel was not mine, but Mansel's, and I will not pick over the blossoms he chose to lay upon the grave.

Without a word, we made our way to the cars, and, taking the first, drove slowly out of the drive and down to the castle gate.

Then Mansel climbed in by the window that had the loose bar, and two minutes later he swung the great leaf open and I drove in.

When I was in the courtyard, I stopped and sounded the horn. Before its echoes had died, a casement of the oratory was opened, and Hanbury put out his head.

"All over," said Mansel simply. "Open the doors."

He was on his way to the guard-room, before I was out of the car, with Tester scrambling before him, agog to prove the promise of so unusual a field.

I followed leisurely, still thinking on the death of Rose Noble and of all that had passed, and trying to believe that the clock in the dashboard of the Rolls was telling the truth when it said that the hour was no more than half-past nine.

So I came to the guard-room and down the winding stair.

The passage door was open, and Mansel was standing in the passage, fronting Adèle. His back was towards me, but I saw that his head was bowed and he had her hand to his lips. The back of her other hand was across her eyes.

And between them and me crouched Casemate framed in the passage doorway, pistol in hand.

I let out a cry that might have been heard in Lass, but, as I did so, he fired, and I saw Mansel stagger a little and then sink down on his knees.

Before Casemate could turn, I had knocked him flat on his face and was kneeling upon his back. Then I took my knife and drove it into his spine.

But the mischief was done.

Mansel was still alive, but the bullet had entered his stomach, and there was death in his face.

9

Full Measure

I shall never forgive myself for forgetting that Casemate was still at large. I had thought of him twice since my rescue—once as I lay by the brook, waiting Mansel's return, and again whilst Mansel was gone to open the castle gate; and each time, before he was back, I had let some other matter thrust Casemate out of my mind.

I have no excuse to offer. It was a monstrous negligence, for which I can never account, though sometimes I strive to believe that Rose Noble's familiar possessed me to let Mansel down.

We bore him into the lovely bedchamber and laid him upon the King's bed.

When we would have taken his coat, he shook his head.

"He's got me all right," he whispered; "so let me be."

I tried to say I was sorry, with the tears running down my face.

But he only smiled.

"Rot," he said gently. "Luck of the battle—that's all."

Upon the great bed sat Adèle, steady-eyed as ever, but very pale. She might have been Eve, as Milton has pictured her, sitting upon the green bank, looking into the pool. Her left arm propped her, and she was sitting sideways, after the way of a child; one ring of the broken handcuffs was still about her slim leg. Her hand was in Mansel's, and their two hands lay in her lap; her beautiful head was bowed, and her eyes never left the eyes of the man she loved.

On his other side lay Tester, close up against his lord. Mansel's left hand was upon him; but, though, I think, he would have licked it, the poor scrap never moved, but lay as still as an image, with his chin on his little paws and his eyes upon Mansel's face.

If the others came and went, I did not notice them; and, after a little, I found the windows open and the doors of the chamber shut.

"Punter and Bunch," said Mansel. "Search them for money and take every penny they've got. Go to Innsbruck and buy them two tickets for London. Give them these and drop them outside the town. Someone must watch them in and see that they go. And the caretakers must be dealt with. Perhaps the 'doctor' will help. It shouldn't be very hard to stop their mouths. But try and mop everything up before you go."

I could only nod; and, when he had seen me do this, he closed his eyes.

If he suffered, he never showed it. Indeed, he seemed well content. And, when Adèle stooped to kiss him, a light that was not of this world came into his eyes.

Once I made to rise and leave them, but, interpreting my movement, Mansel lifted his hand and bade me stay.

So we three waited together, as we had waited together the day before, but this time under a shadow which would not pass....

My eyes stole round the room.

The chamber was full of light, and a broad sash of sunshine was lying athwart the wall. The black oak, the gold and the crimson feasted the eye. The tapestries beckoned into the glades they pictured, and the four men-at-arms about the bed insisted upon the presence they had been set to keep. All I can say is that the presence was there. For once Fate had not bungled, but had laid a king upon a king's bed to die.

Then I thought of Maximilian and of the exquisite surname which he had won, and at last I saw the writing which had been all the time upon the wall.

Destiny will be served. For more than four hundred years that room had been swept and garnished, had stood ever ready and waiting for "The Last of the Knights." Jonathan Mansel, Gentleman, had come into his own.

My eyes returned to the bed—to read as dreadful a message as ever I saw.

We had drawn the coverlet, before we had laid him down, exposing a silken quilt that had, I think, once been white, but was now yellow with age. Upon this there was now a great blood-stain, very slowly spreading about his hips.

The terrible sight shocked me, and I covered my eyes.

Adèle was speaking.

"Can we do nothing, my darling? No single thing?"

Very gently he shook his head.

"If we were in London," he murmured, "they might have a shot; but I'm very comfortable, and it's a great relief to know that we're out of the wood."

A dry sob shook Adèle.

"Another wood's coming, Jonah; it's very near; I must go into that alone—and there aren't any leaves on the trees."

Mansel smiled very tenderly.

"The spring's in your heart, my darling. The trees will break at your coming and the wood will become your bower."

Adèle shook her lovely head.

"Ah, Jonah, I've no heart left. If we could have gone in together, I wouldn't have cared; but it's ... so dreadful, Jonah ... to face it alone."

"Hush, my darling. William will see you through. Think only how rich you made me, that I'm going laden with a treasure which no Customs can take away. Remembering that, my Lady, how can you mourn? See what a tide I'm taking. It's never been half so high in all my life. I'm going out on the very full of the flood, and the ebb that might have hurt me will never run."

"It's our tide you're taking, Jonah—our wonderful, shining tide. And I've got to stand on the shore and see it go down. I could have borne it with you. It never would have fallen, so long as you were beside me—to share our lovely secret and teach me to play the game."

For the first time a troubled look came into his face.

"It's better like this, my sweet. We might have slipped and fallen, or—"

"Never," sobbed Adèle. "You know it. Not if Boy were to live for fifty years. You love me, and that's enough. Your arms have been about me, and I've kissed your blessed lips, and I'd have lived on that memory—"

"Live on it still, my queen. Do me that matchless honour. Lift up the heart I touched, because I touched it, the eyes I kissed, because a man knelt and looked up and saw himself in them."

"Oh, Jonah, if love could do it, it should be done. But it's strength alone that can help me, and all my strength is in you. You don't know your strength, my darling. You carry so lightly what no other man could lift. We've always leaned on you, Jonah; the first thing I learned of Boy was to lean upon you. When they took me that day by Sava, I knew you'd come. I wasn't afraid, because I knew you'd find me and pull me out. I wasn't afraid of Rose Noble—I told him so, I told him he hadn't an earthly and that, if he took me to Hell, you'd follow me down and break him and carry me back. And I wasn't afraid to love you and take your love—to play with the fire of Heaven, for I knew I could count on your strength to bring us through. But now . . . you're going my darling . . . and I must fend for myself. And I'm lost and beggared and beaten, and—oh, Jonah, I'm terribly afraid."

Mansel put up a hand and touched her hair.

"I found my strength in your nature, in the light of your steady, brown eyes and the flash of your smile; in your beautiful voice and your laughter and the play of your little hands; in the lisp of your footfalls and, at last, in the brush of your lips . . . You gave me my strength, my darling; and the spirit that lighted my life can light its own. Two days ago in this room you made me a king—of your own sweet will, though Death had his ear to the keyhole, and Terror his eyes on the latch. That's not the way of fear."

"But you were with me, Jonah. I tell you, with you to lean on, I knew no fear."

"A fiction, my beauty, a fiction. You mustn't bow down to an image that you set up. It wasn't I that set the stars in your eyes or gave that fine, proud curve to your beautiful mouth. Adèle was a great lady, before ever she head my name. So lift up your head, in the old familiar way. Look Fate in the eyes, my darling, and he'll always give you the wall."

Adèle seemed to brace herself. Then she took his hand and kissed it and held it against her heart.

"I'll try," she said quietly. "If Tester will let me, I'll do what I can to help him; and, as soon as we've got our bearings, Tester and I will try."

I saw the dog's ears lift, but he never stirred.

"Poor little chap," said Mansel. "I'm afraid it'll hit him hard."

Then he spoke to the scrap and told him that he must look after Adèle and that soon he was to be her dog, "for you see, old fellow," he murmured. "I've got to go away. And it's not like the other times, for this time . . . I shan't come back."

A tremor ran through the dog's frame, and he gave a little whimper that wrung my heart. As plainly as if he had spoken, he was acknowledging the sentence which the man that he worshipped had passed. Devotion so piteous and so absolute would have drawn tears from any stone, and I was not surprised when beneath this turn of the roller Adèle broke down.

She slipped from the bed to the floor, buried her face in her hands and shook like a leaf.

"I can't face it," she said wildly. "Three days ago I could have done it, but now it's too late. Two days ago the face of my world was changed. We changed it together, Jonah, you and I. But, when we changed it, we set a yoke on our necks... I wouldn't go back for fifty million worlds—our yoke's my pride and glory, the loveliest jewel that ever a woman wore. They were going to tattoo me, Jonah—to write your name on my back. I wish to God they'd done it; but it wouldn't have been the same as the yoke we put on together two days ago. And now I've got to carry... our yoke... alone.... Between us, its weight was nothing. It had no weight. Day and night I'd have worn it, and life would have been the lighter because it was there. But alone, Jonah ... *alone*. How can I lift up my heart, when my fellow is gone?"

Great beads of sweat were standing on Mansel's brow; but his voice, though low, was steady as it had ever been.

"'The one shall be taken,'" he said, "'And the other left.' That is the private touchstone of the great Alchemist himself. Only the greatest hearts come to be put to such a shining proof, and those that pass it, my lady, emerge so tempered that no blow can ever dent them, and they can turn the edge of any sorrow."

Adèle dragged herself up and knelt to the bed; as she leaned over blindly, Mansel put his arm round her neck....

And then, for a while, there was silence, and the whisper of the water, taking its leap from the terrace, was all the sound we heard.

Tester lifted his head and looked at the wall.

At first I could hear nothing; then came a step in the passage, and, an instant later, Hanbury opened the door.

As he looked at the bed—

"Ah, George," said Mansel, and smiled.

Hanbury glanced behind him, and a tall, fresh-faced man came into the room.

"This is Dr. Buchinger," said George. "He is an Innsbruck surgeon, who happened to be at Lass."

The other bowed to Adèle; then he stepped to the bed.

I was just in time to catch Tester, who would have flown at his throat, but the surgeon ignored the flurry and, frowning a little at the blood-stain upon the quilt, stooped to set his fingers on Mansel's wrists.

There was a breathless silence.

Then he took a case from his pocket and straightened his back.

"I must give an injection" he said. "Please see if the room is ready and bring a shutter or something on which you may carry him."

"You see," said George, "it was like this. I knew it was a chance in a million, but there was the car waiting, and the bookseller ready to help. I would have gone to Innsbruck, for I hadn't much hope of Lass. 'Can there any good thing come out of Nazareth?' But my father's a doctor, you know, and I knew we were up against time—hæmorrhage. You don't die of the wound; you die of the loss of blood. I tell you, I had next to no hope....

"All the way I kept wondering how I could smother the rumours my action was going to start. Call in a doctor, and you always open the sluice. When I thought of the flood behind, my foot went out to the brake. It amounted to this—I was putting all our shirts on the rankest outsider that ever was saddled up. Then I thought of the shock his death would be to Adèle and the awful look in your face as we carried him in....

"By the time we ran into Lass, I had a half-baked plan.

"We drove to the local surgeon's. His door was open and, by the grace of God, he was just showing Buchinger out. Then I made a most happy mistake. I took Buchinger for the local, and the local for Buchinger's man. Before the bookseller could stop me, I'd asked if he could speak English, and, when he said 'yes,' I dragged him into the house and started in. There was no time for finesse; my only card was the money, so I jolly well bunged it in. I said if he'd do the case, we'd pay him a thousand pounds—*and another four thousand pounds three months from to-day, provided we'd reason to think that he'd held his tongue*. Then I took out the wallet that Mansel keeps in the car and laid the notes on the table before his eyes. He seemed rather staggered and looked at me very hard. Then the bookseller put in his oar. 'I will give you my word,' he said, 'that there is nothing to fear. This gentleman is saving a lady's name.' That seemed to reassure Buchinger, but still he wouldn't say 'yes.'

"'Dr. Rachel must help me,' he said, and looked at the wallah that I had thought was his man.

"Then I saw my mistake and that he must be another and *bigger* pot.

"'By all means,' said I, and added two hundred and fifty to what there was on the board.

"The two of them looked at the notes.

"Then Rachel made a noise like a siphon and picked his up....

"Well, he has a kind of clinic attached to his house. All the stuff for an operation was ready to hand. Without Buchinger, he'd have been hopeless—forgotten from A to Z. But Buchinger knows his job. He called for paper and pencil and made out a list. When he'd done, he checked it over; then he gave it to Rachel and told him to 'get those things into the car.' Five minutes later we picked him up at a chemist's two streets away."

"You've saved his life," said I.

"That remains to be seen," said George. "But, if I have, it's pure fluke. *Buchinger was leaving the house to catch his train. He was actually on the doorstep.* And Rachel could no more have done it than you or I. Clever enough, no doubt; but take him out of his groove, and he loses his mind."

This estimate, if not exact, was unpleasantly near the truth. As Rachel was bidden, he did—with an excellent grace; but the poor man's composure was gone, and his efforts to bring it to heel were as obvious as they were vain. This made us all fear for his discretion; but the bookseller presently insisted that the sight of familiar surroundings would send this disorder away and that, once he was back in his province, we could count upon his prudence as upon that of a sage.

This comforted us, for there was much to be done, and our cup of anxiety was full.

When the operation was over, Buchinger told us plainly that, so far from his life being saved, Mansel might die any minute during the next three days.

"When he thought he was dying," he said, "he was perfectly right. He was dying—and dying fast. He is now no longer dying; Dr. Rachel and I have stopped that. But he is standing still—on the very edge of death. And there we must try to keep him, for, nothing that I can do can draw him back. If he should live for three days, he will himself draw back; and then a medical student could make him well. But if, before then, he slips—that is the end.

"I shall, of course, stay here. As luck will have it, my holiday does not end for another six days. But Dr. Rachel must go. You will fetch him again this evening, when he will bring my things and some drugs that I want. And, if you will keep your secret, I think I should drive into Lass by some indirect way. Of course, you should have a nurse—two nurses. But women would talk. Only, I fear for the health of that beautiful girl...."

We drew what cheer we could from these solemn words and, since Adèle was with Mansel, turned with relief to the business of setting our house in order as best we might.

Rose Noble lay still unburied, for Carson and Bell had left him and rushed to the castle directly they heard the shot, and, finding the truth so dreadful, had rightly stayed within call. And, since another grave had now to be dug, we put these two matters in train before anything else.

The surgeons had not seen Casemate, for, while George was gone for a doctor, the servants had taken the body into the Dining-room. For this I was thankful, for to help a man out of a trespass is one thing, but to stand accessory to homicide is, as they say, a different pair of shoes.

And here I may sat that, if Rachel was too much bemused, Buchinger was far too wary to ask any questions at all; he must have suspected that Mansel's was not the only blood that had been shed, but he saw the danger of knowledge and held his peace.

When he had returned to the sick-room and George had gone off with Rachel, to drive him to Lass, we carried Casemate's body down to the second car, and Bell and Rowley and I drove up to the wood. And there we laid the fellow to such rest as a murderer has; and I trust he will lie undisturbed for the rest of our days, for, do what we would, we could not withdraw my knife; but were forced to bury the dead with this document fast in his back.

Until these grim rites were over, I could not rest, for, if dead men can tell no tales, a corpse can speak for itself, and I was determined to take no chances at all.

George, who was very soon back, held the same view, and the four of us laboured like fury, until the business was done.

When we left the thicket, we took with us Punter and Bunch and cast them into the kitchen which they had turned into a gaol. When they saw their quarters, the two looked ready to burst; but, if they disliked their fortune, they had only themselves to thank. I do not suppose that hospitality was ever shown so grudgingly or taken so ill, but, though we hated their presence, we thought it wise not to enlarge them until we should leave the castle for good and all.

We then set the caretakers free.

As may be believed, these were half dead of apprehension. Indeed, their one idea was to fly the place, and, but for the bookseller, whom they had known for some years, we should have had no choice but to detain them by force.

Rose Noble, of course, had "bought" them; and, once he was fairly installed, they could not go back. They could not betray his presence, without disclosing that they had betrayed their trust, and obeyed in fear and trembling their new and terrible lord. They had in the end made up their minds to vanish, but he had divined their intention and, coming upon them whilst they were packing some traps, had cuffed their right feet together and locked them into their room. In this miserable state we found them, full of lamentation and the expectation of death and entirely persuaded that, even if they were saved, as the result of their bondage they would be lame for life. Indeed, when we cut the links, they both declared that they could not possibly walk, that the iron had set up gangrene and other faint-hearted rubbish that wearied us all. With infinite patience, however, the bookseller took them to task, and, when he had at last convinced them that they were whole, made it plain that they still had a chance of avoiding such penalties as they had justly earned. At this, they pricked up their ears, and within the hour it was settled that we would repair such damage as might have been done to the house and would hold our tongues, provided they served us truly so long as we stayed. The terms were not to their liking, but, since beggars cannot be choosers, they had to agree, and the woman cooked us some luncheon that very day....

When George drove to Lass, to seek Rachel, that afternoon, he fetched from the inn what few belongings we had left there against our return, and, giving out that Mansel had crushed his foot and lay in a peasant's cabin in danger of losing his leg, sowed the seed of a story for Rachel to tell. Him we took back to a junction some miles below Lass and promised to meet him there at ten the next day.

The bookseller flatly refused to let us convey him at all, maintaining that it was to our interest that he should go as he came and so be forearmed to affirm that, if there was trouble abroad, it was not at the Castle of Gath. His housekeeper, a notorious gossip, was aware that he had intended to visit the castle that day; any perilous rumours, therefore, were sure to be brought straight to him, and, if he was able to disclaim an acquaintance with strife, he would be able to crush them once and for all. His one appearance in the car could be explained well enough; Hanbury had met him at the cross roads, in some distress, and he had offered to show him the surgeon's house.

The debt we owe to that man can never be paid. He had a heart of gold. Most brave, discreet and understanding, he threw himself into our venture, as though it had been his own, and would, I think, have cheerfully gone to the stake, rather than have spoken one word to our embarrassment. We had purchased the surgeons' silence, as well as their skill; the caretakers went in fear; but the bookseller held his tongue and gave of the best he had because he liked us and without, I am sure, any thought of any reward.

By dusk some sort of order had been set up. Rooms had been cleaned and prepared for Buchinger and Adèle; and each of us had his quarters and his particular charge.

That night a note went to Poganec.

I am free and safe and sound—at a terrible cost.
Jonah has been wounded and lies at the point of death.
Adèle

And there he lay for three days, as Buchinger had said, in the room that Adèle had once used in the southwest tower.

Then the mists parted, and they said he would live.

"I think," said Buchinger, "that he will recover fast. If all goes well, he can leave his bed in a fortnight, and in another week you may drive him home. But not before that. To-morrow morning I shall return to Innsbruck, but shall visit him twice in each week until he is well. No doubt you will kindly convey me in one of your cars. Dr. Rachel must still attend him twice a day; but, when a week has gone by, once in the day will do. I have told Miss Adèle that now his servant may very well take the night watch, and, if you do not want another patient upon your hands, I recommend you to insist that this is done."

Here something touched his leg, and we both looked down to see Tester wagging his tail.

"Ah, you monkey. Yes, that is all very well. I come to save your master, and you fly in my face. You are carried off, breathing threatenings and thirsty to drink my blood. And now I have done it in your teeth, I am your very good friend and must be noticed and honoured—"

Tester rolled over and put his paws in the air; and, when the surgeon stooped, jumped up to lick his face.

I never saw the dog so use any other stranger, and he would not look at Rachel, for all his zeal. With this blunt discernment all his conduct was of piece. We had set a box for him in the "gallery of stone," and there he had lain, like a mouse, since the day on which Mansel was hit, never going further than the terrace, the door to which stood open for him to use. He never sought to enter the sick-room, but always rose and listened, whenever the door was opened by day or night, and anxiously scanned the faces of such as went. So for those three black days. After that he went out and about and took his ease and only kept his box when we went to bed. Then came the day when Mansel asked for him; and, when I went to the door, to go and find him, there he was, standing on the threshold, with one paw raised and his eyes seeking confirmation of what he believed to be the truth.

I do not seek to magnify his instinct, but, well as we knew him, these things astonished us all, and, if speech was denied him, he had, I think, another and finer faculty.

There seemed little doubt that, so far, our secret was safe. We drew our supplies, not from Lass, but from towns in other directions from twenty to fifty miles off; since the day of Mansel's wounding, we had not been seen in Lass, and we fetched and carried Rachel by devious ways; when we left the drive, we did so with great circumspection, the castle gates were kept shut, and no lights were shown in the building or on the cars.

George had visited Poganec, had told the most of our story and had explained our case. The question of the Pleydells' coming had naturally arisen at once, but, after a while, they determined to stay where they were. Captain Pleydell could not be moved, because of his leg; and the others decided that, till Mansel was in a condition to be not only prepared for their coming, but satisfied that this move was entailing no risk, their appearance would only concern him and would do no manner of good. So soon, however, as Mansel began to mend, we were to fetch Daphne Pleydell, while it was dark, to spend a day in the castle and go back the following night; a day or so later Major Pleydell would come, and, when these two visits were over, Adèle would visit her husband in just the same way.

That all this precaution was needful, there is no doubt. Lass was big with rumour, and, though much of the gossip was wild, we were astounded to find how close some approached the truth.

Rachel maintained his story that Mansel had crushed his leg, and the bookseller quietly diverted suspicion from Gath; but neither could shut the eyes or stop the ears of the town whose sleep was seldom broken by anything more stirring than a chimney afire or an instance of petty theft.

The bookseller wrote to us daily, always directing his letter to a different village or town, from which we posted our answer, telling how Mansel did.

I cannot do better than make the first letter he wrote us speak for itself.

Sirs,
You shall please take great cares. Your fetchings of

Dr. Rachel cannot be too secretly made. It is said here that a priest is led into the mountains and there destroyed; that one man has met him to appointment in a house of the alley over against my shop and would lead him into the mountains, where three more men were lying ready to kill; that the priest was to seek a woman who had his love and was not of her own mind because she loved him so dearly; that the woman is lying still in his murderer's arms and that these had a great motor-car in which they drove themselves; that such car is now in Welsa, under the village's police, who wait for it to be demanded, but all in vain, because the murderers are afraid; that you came after the priest, to save his life, and are encamped in the mountains until the murderers shall move; that they are shut themselves in one of the castles, but you do not know which, and because of your friend's misadventure, you are at a deadlock. And other things was said, that the woman wears the clothes of a man, that the priest is hanged to death, and many other untruths; but those of above will show upon you how clean you must pick your way.

All this, I learn, was said for two or three days, but was not come to my ears, because I sit still with my books; but, when I return from Gath, I find myself well awaited, and I am glad I was ready with my tale.

I trust and believe your friend is surviving his wound.

Your obedient servant
H.S.

Still the days went by, and no one troubled us; the visits were paid, and the world seemed none the wiser; our curious heritage became a pleasant habit; and Mansel grew steadily better under the love of Adèle.

*　　　*　　　*

I was sitting on the terrace one morning, on a cushion of one of the cars, looking at the exquisite prospect and finding much virtue in sloth, when a hand came to rest upon my shoulder, and there was Adèle.

Care and her vigil had left her a little pale, but this only gave her beauty a delicate look which suited it very well.

Without a word, she sat herself down beside me, propped herself on an arm and tilted her chin.

"Have you drunk your milk?" said I.

"Yes," said Adèle. "Beautiful, fragrant milk—straight from the cow. Who travelled all night to get it—and drinks canned milk himself?"

"George Hanbury," said I.

Adèle sighed.

"I wonder," she said, "I wonder if ever a woman was so well served."

"You must thank yourself," said I.

"So Jonah says," said Adèle; "but I can't see why."

"You must take our word," said I, "for it's gospel truth."

And so it was. Without any thought of favour, we delighted to serve Adèle. I am not quite certain why. It was not because she was more bodily and mentally attractive than any girl that I have ever seen; it was not because of her dignity or because of her natural grace. She had a way with her. This was a royal way, and—it was the way of a child. She was full-grown, she was worldly, she was wise; but, with it all, she had never lost that golden flush of childhood which makes its way directly into the hardest heart. I have often wondered how Rose Noble could have used her so harshly, but I think that he had no heart, and the others, I suppose, had no choice but to follow his monstrous lead.

"Do you remember," she said, "a question you asked me not very long ago?"

"Yes," said I. "'What about going back?'"

She nodded.

"That's right. I think you saw better than I how very hard it would be. It would have been—awfully hard. But Fate's very wise. They say God tempers the wind to the shorn lamb. I'm sure he does—in His mysterious way. I've often wondered how such a thing could be done; but now I know. So soon as the lamb is shorn, he lets the wind blow for a moment *with ice in its breath;* and that moment's so dreadful that ever after that the lamb doesn't feel the wind...And that's our case. It would have been awfully hard. But that half-hour was so dreadful that now the rest seems easy, and I'm not a bit afraid. It's the old question of contrast. I've lifted the load that I might have had to carry. It crushed me—for half an hour. And then for three days and nights I stood waiting to know my fate." She drew a deep breath. "Can you wonder, William, that, after that experience, the future weighs no more than this necklace around my neck?"

"Thank God for that, Adèle."

For a little while she sat silent, smiling into the distance as though there were something there which I could not see.

"I'm very lucky," she said. "My love-affair's been so perfect—from first to last. I was taken because he loved me, and then he came in his strength, to pull me out. I shared the rough with him; and, whilst we were under the shadow, he slept with his head in my lap; when he was hurt, I was there; and alone I've had the glory of helping him back to life. And it's all been out of the world: we've never had to use the back stairs, or whisper, or put out the light. There's been nothing sordid about it, and nothing cheap. And, when it's finished, it'll go, like a painting, into the quiet gallery of which you and he and I have the only keys ."

"I shall often walk there, Adèle."

She nodded gravely.

"I like to think that you will."

There was another silence.

Presently she knitted her brows.

"I'm upset about Boy," she said. "You can't get away from the fact that I'm letting him down. He is so good to me, and I love him so much. He's so proud of me and of Jonah, and he plays such a splendid game. When you took me to Poganec, he was so glad to see me, but they hadn't told him I was coming, because they knew he'd say that I mustn't leave Jonah's side. You can't beat that, can you?"

"As I live," said I, "I believe that he'd understand. Of course, you can't possibly tell him; but, if you did, I believe that he'd understand. So don't be upset, Adèle. It was nobody's fault. It was the most natural thing that ever happened."

Adèle turned a glowing face.

"William, tell me. All the world would say that Jonah and I were doing a rotten thing. How is it you don't think so? How is it you understand?"

"There's no one like him," said I.

"I know, but—"

"And, then—there's no one like you."

"Oh, William...."

"The page and the lady," said I. "It's often happened before. And I shall survive." I rose to my feet. "But that, I think, is the reason why I understand. I can look at him with your eyes, and I can see you with his, and—well, Kings and Queens go together, and, oh, my dear, I'm so glad I shall have that key."

Adèle put out a slim hand, and I lifted her up.

I would have loosed her fingers, but she left them in mine.

"You're a lot like him," she said quietly. "Rowley told me who fetched the milk."

Then she put her hand to my lips.

On the last day we spent at the castle, the bookseller came, by arrangement, to bid us "good-bye."

We made much of him, as was natural, but, when we had talked for a while and he had broken his fast, he begged us to let him ramble from room to room, "for my great desire," he said, "was to make my guide pages more full, and never again shall I have an occasion like this."

So we showed him the trick of the table—which afforded him infinite delight—and then let him go his way, to discover and speculate to his heart's content. Ere it was sundown, he had a great book full of notes, and his voice was trembling with pleasure as he told over his hoard.

Then Mansel took him apart and did the delicate business of making him rich. I do not know what he said or how he said it, but, when it was over, the poor old fellow was quite unable to speak, and, though he shook hands with us all a number of times, and though George and I went with him as far as the porch, he never once opened his mouth, until the wicket stood open and he was about to step out.

Then—

"Sirs," he said shakily, "to some friendships there is no farewells."

Then he clapped his hat on his head and went his way.

We watched him pass up the spur, but, though we

stood ready to wave, he never looked back, and at last the wood swallowed him up and we saw him no more.

When the dusk came in, George, with Bell and Rowley, went off with Punter and Bunch, to take them to Innsbruck, purchase their tickets for London and see them go.

The latter gave no trouble, comported themselves most humbly and touched their hats to their warders, if ever they spoke. Such piety suggested that their recent bodily affliction had chastened their souls; but Rowley, who was watching to see that they took the train, reported that, when they did so, Punter was burdened with a suitcase and Bunch with a dressing-bag, and, since, when they left the car, they had had no luggage and neither had upon him the price of a glass of beer, I fear that they were incorrigible and that honesty was, so to speak, beyond their element.

George was not to return to the castle, but to meet us at midnight at a point between Lass and Villach, some twenty miles from the hog's back from which we had scanned the country a month before. So, when we had dined and the terrier had had his supper, Carson and Tester and I went the rounds for the last time.

No sign of our occupation was anywhere to be seen.

The damage we had done in the antechamber had been repaired, the bullet-holes in the Dining-room had been stopped and such window-glass as was broken had been replaced. The rooms had all been cleaned, the floors shone like glass, the beds had been stripped; the caretakers had such linen as had been used, and this the woman would wash and return to store; what rubbish and litter there was had been taken the night before and sunk in a river we knew of ten miles away.

When we had finished our inspection and found all well, I sent Carson down, with Tester, to finish loading the Rolls, and walked by myself on the roof for half an hour.

The night was lovely, and, though October was in, the air was as still and gentle as that of a summer's eve. A fine moon was riding a cloudless sky and shedding enough pale light to lend the towers and bulwarks a fanciful air and all the world I could see the look of a fairy-tale.

I do not believe in Enchantment; but, if there be such a thing, it stood at my shoulder that evening upon the ramparts of Gath. Castle, spur and thicket, mountains and forests and the flesh of the water below seemed all "such stuff as dreams are made," and I could not shake off the feeling that we were about to quit a fantastic country which, search for it as we might, we never should see again.

When it was ten o'clock, I made my way to the courtyard. There all was in order: what luggage we had was in place, and the rugs and cushions for Mansel were piled in the back of the car.

Then I went to the terrace, as they had asked me to do, to tell Adèle and Mansel that it was time to be gone.

They had left the chairs, set for them, and were standing together up to the balustrade; his arm was about her, and her head was against his shoulder, and the two threw a single shadow upon the flags.

For a moment I stood, irresolute, at the head of the steps. Then I went heavily down....

They did not turn at my coming. Only Adèle stretched out a little hand.

I came and stood beside her, and her arm went about my shoulders and held me close.

So we stood, all three together, looking unto the hills....

Mansel was speaking.

"The very elements respect you," he said. "Was ever a night so lovely, to round a dream?"

"Our dream," breathed Adèle. "Our beautiful, shining dream. You gave it us, darling. By keeping my letters, you gave it. And your strength has been its glory, your gentleness its life."

"You wrote the letters," said Mansel. "Because of that, I loved them so very much. I never thought I should burn them...But then I never thought that, in their place you would give me something—something that won't go into words, Adèle, that all the ages must envy me, and that no thieves can steal."

Adèle's arm left my shoulders and came to rest upon his.

"Oh, Jonah—my love, my darling."

Mansel held her close, looking down on her upturned face.

"I love you," he said. "I love the stars in your eyes and the breath of your lips. I love your hair and your temples and the pride of your exquisite mouth. I love all your peerless beauty. But, most of all, my queen, I love your darling nature and the finest, bravest heart that ever closed a book at the end of one golden chapter—and put it back on the shelf."

He kissed her steadily, and I covered my eyes....

Adèle turned to me and put her arms round my neck.

"Dear William," she said, "you saw the beginning, and now you see the end. You've been with us in light and in shadow; you've given us freely the best that a man can give; and I can only tell you that the love that you have shown us is part and parcel of our dream."

With that, she put up her lips to be kissed, like a little child, and I kissed them a little fearfully, for my clay is common, but she and Mansel were spirits of another sort.

Then she returned to her lover, and I left them to the rustle of the water and the pale splendour of the moonlight and the motionless plumage of the opposing hills....

Very soon they came up to the "gallery of stone," and I shut the door behind them and followed them down to the courtyard, without a word.

Five minutes later the Rolls stole up the spur and into the wood.

On the following day George Hanbury and I would have returned to Villach, if not to Town; but this Mansel would not hear of, and, when he discovered our proposal, Adèle and his cousins rose up in pleasant indignation against our leaving their roof.

We could not withstand such goodwill, but, while George was glad to give way, I was reluctant, and, indeed, I shrank from the visit, I think, with cause.

I need have had no fear.

We stayed at Poganec until October was old; every day was of summer, and, though the leaves changed colour, they did not begin to fall. But things other than the season were cordial, and the weeks I had dreaded so turned to my relief that, when we drove back to London, I was in higher feather than I had been for months.

Adèle and Mansel took up the thread of life as though they had never let it fall. If ever they made believe, I never saw it; and, when I was alone with either, neither by word nor look was any reference made to what had passed between them at the Castle of Gath. Indeed their passionate adventure might never have been. The old, easy relation was back in its seats; they were content—happy, for all the world to see; they avoided no ground, because to them it was tender; where others' fancy took them, thither they went, riding so straight and unconcernedly that I, behind them, caught something of their courage and found the formidable fences of no account.

I think this will show how very fine was their temper, how brave and notable their style. Handsome in all they did, in this supreme ordeal they gave full measure, and I like to think that with that same full measure it shall one day be measured to them again.

Not for some days did I remember that we had never replaced the stone slab which had sealed the entrance to the Closet from the archway below.

This will be found one day, where it lies beneath the King's bed; and one day the coverlet will be drawn, and men will find the blood-stain upon the quilt.

What curious interest will not these things arouse? The name of Maximilian will be in every mouth. Old annals will be re-read, old narratives revised and legends brought to bed of fine new tales of wrath and mischief and murder saved or done. And yet I cannot think that, for all their bravery, they will compare with the truth.

This I am never weary of recalling, and many a winter's night I have sat at Maintenance, looking into the fire of logs and giving my memory rein.

Our desperate drive to Poganec, and the red of Mansel's taillight flicking into and out of sight; the roar of the waterfall, and the high-pitched laugh of the rogue that played with Mansel and lost his game; my perilous journey upon the roof of the car, and the first, stupendous survey of the Castle of Gath; our stealthy entry into the King's Closet, the ominous creek of the floorboard and then the frantic pounding upon the door; Rose Noble at the head of the table, and Mansel's lightning move, and the crash of the shots; our vigil by the open window, and the enemy's hideous laughter floating into the night; Casemate's halting footfalls, and Mansel asprawl upon the terrace, with the rope by his side; and, then, the death of Rose Noble, and Mansel on his knees in the passage, with Adèle, aghast and piteous, holding him up. . . .

The remembrance of these things is precious to me, for I had my part in them, and the tapestry they make belongs to that quiet gallery of which Mansel and Adèle and I have the only keys.